NAPPANEE P...
NAPPAN... IN 46550

"Grow up!"

"Maybe you didn't ask for any help," Drew continued tersely, "but you got it. Why can't you just accept it gracefully instead of storming in here like some sort of she-demon with a vendetta against any man who takes an interest in her?"

"Because I'm not interested in your interest!" Sabrina cried. "Nor your insults!"

"Why don't you own up to your feelings, Sabrina? It's no crime to have them. Why are you fighting me—and yourself?"

"Let me go!" she cried, wrenching her arm free. "I don't know what you're talking about."

"Yes, you do," he said, and the smoldering intensity of his gaze was frightening.

Then his lips covered hers. He grasped her wrists, pulling her hands out to bring her body full up against his as his mouth plundered the hidden riches of hers, hungrily. His hands slid slowly up her arms to her shoulders as their kiss deepened, grew wilder in its savage sweetness . . .

Dear Reader:

By now our new cover treatment—with larger art work—is familiar to you. But don't forget that, in a sense, our new cover reflects what's been happening *inside* SECOND CHANCE AT LOVE books. We're constantly striving to bring you fresh and original romances with unexpected twists and delightful surprises. We introduce promising new writers on a regular basis. And we aim for variety by publishing some romances that are funny, some that are poignant, some that are "traditional," and some that take an entirely new approach. SECOND CHANCE AT LOVE is constantly evolving to meet your need for "something new" in your romance reading.

At the same time, we *haven't* changed the successful editorial concept behind each SECOND CHANCE AT LOVE romance. We work hard to make sure every romance we publish is a satisfying read. And at SECOND CHANCE AT LOVE we've consistently maintained a reputation for being a line of the highest quality.

So, just like the new covers, SECOND CHANCE AT LOVE romances are satisfyingly familiar—yet excitingly different—and better than ever.

Happy reading,

Ellen Edwards

Ellen Edwards, Senior Editor
SECOND CHANCE AT LOVE
The Berkley Publishing Group
200 Madison Avenue
New York, N.Y. 10016

P.S. Do you receive our SECOND CHANCE AT LOVE and TO HAVE AND TO HOLD newsletter? If not, be sure to fill out the coupon in the back of this book, and we'll send you the newsletter free of charge four times a year.

PILLOW TALK

LEE WILLIAMS

A
SECOND CHANCE AT LOVE
BOOK

Other Second Chance at Love Books by
Lee Williams

STARFIRE   #189

PILLOW TALK

Copyright © 1984 by Lee Williams

All rights reserved. No part of this publication may be reproduced or
transmitted in any form or by any means, electronic or mechanical,
including photocopy, recording, or any information storage and retrieval system, without permission in writing from the publisher.

Requests for permission to make copies of any part of the work should
be mailed to: Permissions, Second Chance at Love, The Berkley Publishing Group, 200 Madison Avenue, New York, NY 10016.

First edition published September 1984

First printing

"Second Chance at Love" and the butterfly emblem are trademarks
belonging to Jove Publications, Inc.

Printed in the United States of America

Second Chance at Love books are published by
The Berkley Publishing Group
200 Madison Avenue, New York, NY 10016

To Dee-Ann Mernit,
without whom this wouldn't be, and to Richard and John Michael and Susan W. Mernit,
the great supporters.

And in loving memory of Estelle—
who I believe would have enjoyed "this sort of thing."

1

"HELLO, IS THIS Evans Speaker Resources?"

"Yes," Sabrina said, the receiver tucked between her neck and her shoulder as she rummaged about on her cluttered desk, searching for the file that had been there minutes earlier.

"I want to know if you people carry—" The man paused, then recited laboriously, "Tonkyo Dynamic Speaker Cabinets."

Sabrina sighed. "I'm sorry, we're a women's speaker bureau, not a hi-fi outlet."

"Speaker bureaus? You sell furniture?"

Where *was* the damned file? She scanned the floor under the chair by her window. "We don't sell anything," she told the caller absently. "We book women for speaking engagements."

"You're kiddin'," he said in a broad, Brooklynese jeer. "Who pays women to talk?"

"Try Crazy Eddie's," Sabrina snapped tersely, and hung up. She shouldn't have been answering the phone anyway, but Carrie, the usually reliable secretary-receptionist, had called in sick. At a few minutes past noon Sabrina was beginning to wish she had done the same.

The morning's mounting succession of disasters had begun at home, with the mysterious expiration of her trusty alarm clock. Her mad rush to get dressed after oversleeping was halted by the disappearance of her favorite earrings, which showed up at the last minute in her wicker laundry basket—her cat Van Dyke's idea of fun and games. Then, as if on cue, all the taxis in Manhattan conspired to avoid her block. When Sabrina finally made it to the office, Lydia was doing her best impersonation of an irate boss, seeming not at all the kindly middle-aged company president she usually was. The receptionist's absence had been compounded by their newly installed intercom system going newly on the fritz and taking out one of their two phone lines as well.

So it was with some trepidation now that Sabrina knocked on the wall that divided her office from Lydia's.

"Yes?" came Lydia's gravelly voice.

"I can't seem to find the Armstrong file," she called. "Are you sure you don't have it?"

"It was on *your* desk, dear," said Lydia. Sabrina flinched inwardly at the subtle but withering intonation on the *dear*. She hurriedly scanned her desk again, hearing the squeak and scrape of Lydia's chair signal the older woman's approach. The Armstrong people had lost their copy of Sally Rivers's travel arrangements, and as she was due to speak at their meeting in Palm Springs that evening, they were understandably panicked.

"I promised them we'd call back with Sally's itinerary within the hour," Lydia said ominously. She was standing in the doorway, her arms folded, the ever-present cigarette in hand, as Sabrina straightened up from a desperate search of the floor. Lydia's myopic gaze over the top of her bifocals at her junior partner and vice-president was stern.

"It couldn't have vanished into thin air," Sabrina said helplessly. "And no one's been in here but—" She stopped, realization hitting her with a jolt, then grabbed the phone with one hand, the Rolodex with the other as Lydia's eyebrows arched in surmise.

"CBS? Extension one-oh-four-one-one, please." Vanessa Brown, the television anchorwoman, had just stopped by their office to look at a contract for an upcoming booking.

"She left her bag and some folders on my desk when she was talking to you," Sabrina told Lydia, cupping the receiver. "She must've picked up the file by accident when she— Yes?" Vanessa's newsroom secretary was on the line. She informed Sabrina that Vanessa hadn't returned from Evans's, and was out for lunch. Sabrina hung up, stymied, but only for a moment. "She's eating at Dominique's," she exclaimed. "I remember her saying she was going there from here."

Lydia exhaled a little cloud of smoke. "Call them."

Vanessa had just arrived at the restaurant. But as the maître d' went to bring her to the phone, Sabrina realized that the information they needed from the Armstrong folder was extensive—and filed among other papers concerning Sally Rivers that Vanessa, another client, shouldn't really peruse.

"I'm going to pick it up from her," she told Lydia after a brief conversation with Vanessa, who had already discovered she had the file and was about to call Sabrina. "I'll be right back," she added, throwing on her coat. "It's just across town."

Just across town, Sabrina observed grimly, had been too optimistic a phrase. True to the tenor of her Monday thus far, she was gridlocked in a traffic jam, still fifteen blocks from her destination, nearly a half hour later.

With a sigh of frustration she sat back in the cab and opened her compact, examining her face in the little mirror. Her full red lips, long lashes, and slightly hooded eyelids over hazel-brown eyes didn't need touching up. But she applied some rose blush to the soft, pale skin of her cheeks. In Sabrina's eyes the lack of strong cheekbones was a major disappointment. No amount of dieting brought them out; she was cursed with a round, nonangular face—"Infinitely pinchable," Wayne had said. One more reason to relegate the man to the dark recesses of memory. Hadn't he said the same of her perfectly straight and slender nose once?

Sabrina sighed, checking the pins that held her long, thick chestnut-brown hair up in a bun behind her head. She should have shot Wayne, not merely divorced him. She was smoothing back her wavy bangs when the cab lurched into motion. At last they were making up for lost time.

Dominique's was a fashionable celebrity watering hole on the Upper West Side. As she got out of the cab, Sabrina was glad that she'd managed to pull together a dressy enough outfit even in her morning's haste: a man-tailored red wool blazer over a blouse of white lace with ruffled collar and cuffs, a velvet ribbon at the neck, and a pencil-slim black skirt.

The interior of the genteel, softly lit restaurant was all pastel blues, with white-clothed round tables sporting pink flower centerpieces. There was a steady hubbub of urbane voices pitched in murmurs of witty conversation or more boisterous laughter. The people that she saw as she surveyed the room were impeccably groomed, many tanned, all well heeled. Sabrina's heart gave a little tug as her stomach quietly whimpered in counterpoint. Now, now—the filet-mignon days will have to wait, she reminded herself. You made that decision: none of Father's money, none of Wayne's. You'll get here, girl, and on your own steam; no male assistance required, thank you.

The maître d' was engaged in talking to a steward by the bar. Sabrina stepped down the main aisle, anxiously scanning the tables. No Vanessa in sight. She made a complete visual circle of the room. Had she been that late? She was stifling a groan of disappointment when she felt someone's eyes upon her. She turned instinctively to the table on her left.

The eyes that met hers were a soft, gleaming turquoise blue. Their gaze was penetrating, hypnotically direct. She felt pulled into the depths of a devastatingly handsome face, perhaps the most handsome she'd ever seen. Sabrina stared, as if in suspended animation, at his bushy black eyebrows, his aquiline nose, and fine line of lips over shiny white teeth. She admired the firm set of his jaw, the richly tanned skin, the thick, wavy, but perfectly cut jet-black mane of hair. One thin, sexy streak of silver-gray hair curled through the wave swept back from his high forehead. She noted his lean but supple body in a tan suit, powder-blue shirt, and maroon tie. Her eyes were drawn back to his eyes of soft velvet warmly caressing hers.

And then she came abruptly to her senses. The man was assessing her with undisguised interest, his firm but sensuous lips slowly widening in an appreciative smile. Whoops—her mistake. Her lingering gaze had ignited an all-too-familiar predatory gleam in his eye.

Why was it that if a woman looked at any man on the island of Manhattan for more than a fraction of a second, he assumed he'd made an instant conquest? Perhaps it was an innate West Coast versus East Coast prejudice she still harbored, but it seemed to Sabrina that the males on her native San Franciscan stomping grounds hadn't been quite so egocentric. She steeled herself for the inevitable come-on.

"Hello, there," the man said in a deep rumble of a voice. "You look like the woman I've been waiting to meet."

Sabrina sighed. She wasn't in the mood for this. The day had been complicated and exasperating enough already, and her trip across town seemed to have been for naught. She gave this attractive stranger her best turn-to-stone stare.

"I've heard a few," she told him dryly, "but that's the oldest line I've come across in ages."

He was still smiling, deflecting her turn-to-stone stare with disarming ease. If anything, his blue eyes seemed to brighten, the wattage they radiated increasing. Sabrina had the odd feeling she'd just begun some silent will-testing match with a Zen master. She concentrated a steely look of zero-degree intensity back at him.

"That may be so," the man was saying amiably. "But you *do* look like her—only even more attractive than I could have imagined. Have a seat," he offered. "I've got what you came here for."

The arrogance, the smug complacency, the gall of this obnoxious creature inflamed her. "You can wait for a million years," she said evenly, her voice dripping venom. "Whatever you've got is the last thing I'd want, I can assure you." She turned on her heel as he started to rise.

"Wait—" he began.

"Forget it," she muttered, and stalked up the aisle. The maître d' greeted her with a look of polite concern.

"Can I help you, mademoiselle?"

"I was hoping to meet an acquaintance of mine here," she said. "Vanessa Brown. Did she by any chance leave a—?"

The man was already nodding. "Yes, yes, of course," he said, and suavely conducted her back in the direction she'd just come from. They were stopping, Sabrina realized, with growing horror, at the table where the man with the distingué silver streak of hair was seated, imperturbably drinking his coffee. The maître d' indicated the empty seat opposite him with a gracious smile. The man looked up.

"Hello, there," he said in as friendly a tone as before.

Sabrina felt as if she'd stepped into some bizarre waking nightmare. "No," she said, turning to the maître d'. "Vanessa Brown. I'm here to see—"

"Yes, yes," the Frenchman smiled. "Her table." He pulled the chair out for her. Sabrina sat down slowly, feeling her cheeks burn under the man's bland gaze. When the maître d' had departed, she looked up.

"Well," he said, glancing at his watch, "time flies, doesn't it? A million years—" He snapped his fingers. "Just like that."

"All right," she said sharply. "No need to rub it in. I guess I owe you an apology."

He shrugged. "Don't bother. Vanessa had to leave early—some crisis at the newsroom, and she left this with me"—he produced the black file from beneath the table and held it up— "for you, I believe. The last thing you'd want?"

"Yes," she said quickly. "I mean, no. May I?"

She reached for the folder, but the man placed it to his right, beyond her grasp. "In lieu of an apology, would you join me for a cup of coffee? Or a drink?"

She looked at him, and was drawn in again by those magnetic eyes. The blush had left her cheeks, but she still felt hot as he returned her gaze, a slight smile playing on his sensual lips. His physical intensity was unnerving. "No," she said, and continued as though she were a record played at the wrong speed. "I'm really in a hurry to get back to my office."

Damn that smile of his. Her own lips were twitching involuntarily under the force of its seduction. "Your office," he repeated, his eyes caressing hers. "You work with Lydia Evans? You're Sabrina—"

"Hamilton," she supplied. He was offering his hand.

"Drew Dalton," he said.

The name had a familiar ring, though she couldn't place it. Thought was next to impossible for the next moment as she shook his hand. Tiny tremors of pleasure were coursing through her at the feel of his warm, soft skin against hers. For a lingering instant her captivated hand played dumb, resisting her mental commands to let go. Then, with a supreme effort of concentration, she withdrew it from his cocoonlike grasp. Her palm tingling, Sabrina cleared her throat and tried to collect her wits.

"Maybe you'd like to eat something," he was saying. "It seems a shame that you've come all the way across town only to leave Dominique's with an empty stomach."

"No, thanks. I—"

"You're not hungry?"

"Why, do I look it?"

He nodded. "When you came in I said to myself, here's a beautiful woman—that was my first thought—who could probably do with a leisurely meal and some fine wine."

"It's not a leisurely kind of day," she said dryly.

"A rough one so far, eh?" He looked at her with some concern. "Say, does your head hurt?"

She stared at him. "No." Those brilliant blue eyes were truly disconcerting.

"Doesn't it feel uncomfortable, all scrunched up like that?" He was indicating her hair.

"No," she repeated. "Listen—"

"Fantastic hair," he murmured. "It must feel better when you wear it loose."

"No. Well, yes. Mr. Dalton—"

"Drew."

"I really do have to be going," she told him, and added, indicating the black folder tucked under his elbow, "Would you—?"

He was gesturing the waiter over. "I'll walk out with you," he said smoothly.

Though she meant to protest, she was forced to sit by while he quickly paid the check with a credit card. Grabbing the folder from him and beating a hasty exit would be unseemly, though she was sorely tempted. Her antennae were up, wildly registering danger signals: Manipulative male, Grade A, she noted—proceed with caution and don't give him an inch.

She kept her distance as they walked up the aisle. As he left her side briefly to collect his coat, she registered another impression: Drew Dalton appeared to generate an invisible electromagnetic field. The heads of women and men alike turned to look at him as he passed. The man radiated power, and though he was only a few inches taller than she, which made him less than six feet, he seemed to tower over her as he held the door open. They stepped out onto the street.

Sabrina went immediately to the curb, hailing an invisible cab. There were none in sight. She felt Drew watching her as she scanned the street. When she glanced back at him she saw that his eyes were traveling swiftly over her body, appraising her from ankles to earrings. She suddenly felt she was standing at the corner of Columbus and Sixty-seventh without a stitch of clothing on.

"Which way are you headed?" he asked.

Sabrina took the gamble that he wouldn't be going eastward. "Sixty-fifth and East End."

His eyes widened in such complete surprise that she wondered if her address had somehow come out of her mouth in Swahili. "That's where your office is?" he asked, incredulous.

"I know it's mainly residential there by the river." She shrugged. "But it's close enough to midtown for us."

"I'll be damned," he muttered, shaking his head, and then added for no reason she could comprehend, "It's fate."

Abruptly he stepped in front of her, his arm raised, and a Checker cab materialized as if out of thin air. Drew opened the door for her and Sabrina got in. She turned to collect her file from him and say good-bye, then realized, confused, that he was getting in with her. "East Sixty-fifth and the river," he told the driver, shut the door, and leaned back, looking at Sabrina with a contented smile, as if it were his birthday and she was a present.

"Wait a minute," she said as the cab moved into traffic. "I don't really need door-to-door service—just that file," she said pointedly, gesturing at the folder under his arm. "Don't you have someplace else to go?"

He smiled, shaking his head. "I'm going where you're

going," he said. "Here." He handed her the file.

Sabrina took it, looked back at him, felt the waves from his eyes bathe her in a warm appreciative glow, and backed away from him a few inches on the seat. He certainly was the persistent sort. "You have business on the East Side?" she ventured.

He nodded. Sabrina sat stiffly and looked straight ahead. She could hear his relaxed breathing and feel his body heat. She was aware of his masculine scent, a clean, musky mixture of soaped skin and aftershave. Her body was reacting to his in an unfamiliar way. It was as if her normal protective shield mechanism had jammed, and the air between them was alive with freewheeling, zinging electrical impulses.

"What is it that you do?" she asked him, half expecting to learn he was an expert in psychokinetics, who could levitate small objects at will.

"Well, I guess you could say I give advice."

"Really? And who do you give advice to?"

Drew furrowed his brow in reflection. "AT&T, IBM, Exxon...and a bunch of other corporations with lots of initials," he said. "I'm a management consultant."

"Only to small fish, I see," she joked, impressed. Some of the women they handled at Evans were management consultants, but even their most prominent business speakers couldn't reel off the names he had as credits. "So I suppose you hold seminars around the country?"

He nodded. "And I write a little."

Drew Dalton. Suddenly the name and the profession clicked into sharp focus. He wrote a little? The man sitting next to her in his cab was probably collecting thousands of dollars with each click of the taxi's meter. His book, *One Minute to Success,* was the number-one best-selling hardcover book in America. Rumor had it that one could feed the entire population of an impoverished nation with the whopping figure its paperback sale had commanded.

"You're Drew Dalton," she said, instantly aware that it

was not the most intelligent thing she could have said.

"And you're Sabrina Hamilton," he answered, as though she were either a slow learner or an amnesiac. "What are you doing for dinner tonight?"

"I'm not doing," she said, and felt her cheeks color. "I mean, no, thank you. I'm engaged."

"No!" he said, with a look of concern. "To whom?"

Sabrina shook her head. "I'm busy," she said emphatically.

His face brightened. "But unmarried."

A lie was tempting, but something told her he was just the sort of man to follow up. "Yes," she admitted, sighing.

"That's fine," he said happily. "So what do you like, then—Italian? Japanese? French?"

She stared at him.

"Food," he prompted.

"No," she said. "I'm working late. We have a lot of catching up to do at the office."

"I'll bet you do," he said. "Well, perhaps tomorrow night?"

She shook her head. Add monomaniacally aggressive to manipulatively macho, she told herself. Then what he'd just said struck her anew.

"What do you mean, you bet I do?"

"I'm not surprised you have catching up to do. It seems to me you're running that office with chewing gum and rubber bands."

"How do you—" she began indignantly.

"I took a quick peek at your file after Vanessa left." He shook his head ruefully. "Organizing systems like that file are as obsolete as Model T's. I'd say, based on the way you keep track of your information—"

"And what do you suggest?" she interrupted icily.

"Computerize it," he said.

"We're looking into the Telestarter system," she began. "We're planning to order terminals within—"

He was shaking his head. "Forget the Telestarter. It's user-friendly, but slow on the uptake. For the kind of business you're doing, I'd recommend—"

"I think it's possible that I may know a bit more about our particular needs than you do," she said.

He raised an eyebrow. "Well, I've made a few speeches myself."

"I'm sure you make plenty," she said crossly, resenting his smugness all the more. Men like Drew Dalton personified the very problem she and her clients faced. Even though more and more women now held prominent positions in business—a handful of their clients were vice-presidents of large corporations—the men in business associations throughout the country still resisted listening to a woman tell them what to do. Often an account would refuse to consider a woman for a major speaking engagement—even if she was a celebrity—and pick a Drew Dalton instead.

"Actually," he was saying slowly, stretching his legs out as the cab slowed for a light, "I get literally thousands of invitations. But I turn ninety-five percent of them down."

Sabrina looked away from the outline of lean, muscular legs his tight trousers revealed. "Why? Don't tell me you're the shy type."

He grinned, those perfect white teeth gleaming. "No. But my agent has this crazy idea that the time I might spend on a podium would be better used for writing—and I'd have to agree. I don't know if I've mastered the art of public speaking just yet, and most of what I've got to say is in the books anyway. I'm in the middle of researching a new one."

Browsing through a bookstore some months back, Sabrina had picked up his best seller and glanced through it. She'd been shocked to see that the fifteen-dollar tome was a mere hundred pages long, with large print and wide margins. The contents on quick perusal had seemed to her no more than a few simplistic homilies that anyone with a thimbleful of insight had probably already mastered in his business dealings. Though the title alluded to a system Dalton had devised for better management, she'd assumed it meant the book took all of a minute to digest—and probably had taken him only a bit more time to write.

"What's the new book called? *Thirty Seconds to Megabucks?*"

His grin broadened. "Cute," he said. "But wrong. I'm exploring new subjects."

She didn't care to find out what, and his continual exploration of her face was setting her teeth on edge. She merely nodded and looked out the window. Mercifully they were nearing the river.

"Who handles your publicity?" he asked suddenly.

"We do," she admitted.

"Who's your most famous client?"

"Nan Flanders." The syndicated advice columnist was a household name.

"What's her fee?"

"Eight to ten thousand."

"And the percentage you charge an account that hires her?"

Sabrina hesitated.

"I'd guess twenty," Drew said. He squinted at the cab's ceiling, then looked back at her. "I get fifteen thousand a night. Think you could book me? Maybe I'd consider signing on."

Sabrina's mouth dropped open. She shut it, then smiled. "I'm sure I could, but I wouldn't."

"Why not?"

"Evans Speaker Resources is a *women's* speaker bureau. We don't take on male clients."

It was his turn to register shock. "But that's crazy," he said. "You're cutting your own throats."

"We don't think so," she said coolly.

"Not only crazy, but bad business," he went on. "It's counterproductive, and, above all, sexist."

Sabrina felt her blood's temperature rise from simmer to boil. *"We're* sexist?" she began. "Listen, mister, if you think there's anything wrong—"

"Absolutely. If you want to succeed in the modern business world—"

"... with supporting a blighted minority of outstanding women that men like you—"

"—you're going to have to face the realities of interdependence between men and women—"

"... are determined to shut out of prominent positions—"

"—at every level of commerce and communication."

"... then you should look in the mirror if you're looking for sexism! And besides—"

"What's the *number* on Sixty-fifth Street?"

The cab driver's baritone cut through their raised voices. Sabrina turned to the window. They were almost at the end of the block, just yards from her door. "This is fine," she said angrily, thrusting her hand into her pocketbook. "Pull over." She lunged to intercept Drew, who was in the act of taking money out of his wallet, and brandished a ten-dollar bill at the driver.

"Really," Drew began mildly, "you don't have to—"

"I can pay my own way," she said tersely. "I always have." Then she opened the door and quickly scrambled from the cab. "A pleasure to meet you," she called caustically over her shoulder, with the slam of the cab door for punctuation.

She made it as far as the entrance to her building, her heart pounding madly, when she realized, with a sinking sensation, what she'd forgotten. Sabrina stopped, counted to ten, then turned and walked stiffly back to the cab. Drew was standing by his open door, perfectly composed. Sabrina stopped in front of him and silently put out her hand. Drew, poker-faced, handed her the file. She nodded a polite thanks, and he gave her a courtly nod back, with just the faintest hint of mockery. It was enough to make her nearly mangle the file, her hands tightening into fists as she walked away. She didn't look back.

When she reached the top floor she was greeted by two telephone repairmen in overalls, drilling holes in the wall by the elevator in a shower of dust and cacophony.

"All the lines are out!" Lydia called over the din from the doorway, looking harried and tense. "What took you so long?" Something about Sabrina's demeanor stopped her in mid-complaint. "Well, we can't call anyone for a few minutes anyway," she said. Taking the file from Sabrina, she gave her an affectionate pat on the shoulder. "Thanks."

Sabrina nodded and walked into her little office. There were some messages by the phone in Lucy the part-time bookkeeper's cursive but eminently legible hand. Lee Orloff, the meeting planner from the United Apparel Association, had called—that was important. She couldn't reach the Armstrong people yet either. Sabrina sighed and stepped to her window.

The cab was nowhere in sight on the street below. She wondered briefly where that insufferable man had been heading. No matter; he was gone, and that was good. Something about the way he'd completely captivated her, thrown her off-guard at first, disturbed her deeply. Men like Drew Dalton—and, similarly, Wayne, before him—were nothing but trouble. She'd thought she was beyond being attracted to such handsome know-it-alls. Well, she could only hope he didn't often frequent this part of town.

Idly Sabrina's eyes panned up the building opposite, coming to a rest on the imposing penthouse one floor above them. The edifice both awed and irked her. What indulgence! It was truly a house, three stories high, that some rich and enterprising soul had had constructed on the roof of a luxury co-op building, one of its sides facing the river. It was a beautiful, ultramodern building of gray stucco and glinting glass, stunning in both its execution and audacity. Sabrina's little studio apartment on the West Side would probably fit into the penthouse's kitchen.

She and Lydia often wondered at the identity of the man they sometimes glimpsed within, who they'd nicknamed Mr. Penthouse. They tried to figure out why he'd chosen to fashion this imposing high-tech castle in the sky here at the edge of the city, when it would have been well suited for the beach in the Hamptons.

As she watched, the penthouse's inhabitant was visible in his living room. He was approaching the wall-length vertical picture window that faced hers. Sabrina froze as he came right up to it. He was looking at her building, and even at this distance she could see his eyes shift up to meet hers directly. Even at this distance she could watch the smile of recognition form on his handsome face, see him wave a silent greeting.

Drew Dalton was saying hello again.

2

FRESH FROM THE shower at a few minutes past eight, Sabrina stood before her mirror, running a brush through her long, thick mane of hair. Her inner alarm had woken her even earlier than usual, as if to make up for the real clock's mechanical failure the previous morning. Her sleep had been restless, full of vivid dreams whose images hovered at the hazy periphery of her consciousness. Closing her eyes, relaxed and luxuriating in the feel of the brush's gentle pull through the chestnut tresses, Sabrina tried to remember.

There had been a man. His face was indistinct, but even now she could see—and feel—his hands. The fingers were slender, the backs of the tanned, smooth-skinned hands dusted with a fine spray of thin dark hair. His palms had been warm and soft; his touch, gentle but strong...

A warm tendril of arousal was unfurling in her loins.

Sabrina's eyes opened as she remembered what those hands had done, and the pleasure her phantom lover had given her. Facing her naked reflection, she saw her own hand caught in the act of sliding along the hollow beneath her full, pear-shaped breasts, fingers curving up to graze one quivering dark nipple. She met her own eyes in the mirror then, still hooded with sleep.

It has been a while, hasn't it?

Sabrina cleared her throat, her hand falling to her side.

Well, you're allowed to be lonely, aren't you?

Sabrina sighed. Then, gripping the brush firmly, she dragged the mass of shoulder-length hair around the back of her head and began to secure it in a smooth, tightly knotted bun. Quickly and efficiently she fastened it with the hairpins she kept in an antique glass jam jar on the sink, trying to ignore the sudden ache of longing that threatened to disrupt her morning routine.

It wasn't Wayne she missed, she knew that; her love for him had begun its slow death within the one and only year of their abortive marriage. But she sensed that her unconscious knew full well the truth her rational mind struggled daily to repress: The single life she'd chosen to live was turning out to be tough going. She'd thought she could do without men, but there were things a woman's body—and soul—needed . . .

Sabrina had a healthy enjoyment of sex. Ironically it had been the last remaining good thing in her relationship with Wayne. All too often the eroticism of a sultry San Franciscan night in his arms had blinded her to the deeper problems they were having. Their physical rapport had given them the illusion of closeness until the time their greater differences could no longer be ignored.

Sighing, she wondered if good sex and real love came together only in the movies. Her experience had taught her that confusing the former with the latter could be disastrous. Her hair in place, she ran a comb through her wavy bangs. Applying makeup, she forcibly turned her thoughts to the

day ahead. Return that call to Orloff first thing, she reminded herself: His association had some important meet-
ings coming up. Getting a booking for one would be a major
breakthrough.

Her phone was ringing. That was unusual this early.
Sabrina hurried from her little bathroom, throwing on a
towel. Van Dyke, a white, graceful animal, was already at
the phone by her platform bed in the corner of the studio.
His ears pointed straight up. His one green eye and one
blue one fixed on the object of the offensive noise with an
affronted stare. Sabrina smoothed the cat's bristling fur and
picked up the receiver.

"Hello?"

"Sabrina? You're awake?"

At the sound of her father's familiar sandpaper voice,
Sabrina sat down on the bed, stiffening her posture. "Of
course I'm awake, Father," she told him dryly. "I'm a
working woman. I keep the same hours as you do."

"Do you, sweetheart?" he said. His next words were
slightly garbled by the long distance connection. "—five-
thirty here, and I'm off to the tennis courts before I reach
the bank. I don't suppose they have any outdoor courts on
that concrete island of yours?"

"To what do I owe this unexpected call?" she asked,
ignoring his inevitable swipe at the East Coast.

"So it's still like that, eh?" he said, chuckling. "Why are
you always so formal with your old man?"

"Get to the point, Father. I am on my way to *work.*"

"Well, I received your—I wouldn't really call it a letter.
The point is, you sent my check back."

"As I always do," she reminded him. This year his birthday gift had been more insultingly generous than usual.
Ever since she had struck out on her own, her father had
been trying to bribe away her independence, and she wanted
no part of his "help." She blamed him for the family rift
that had traumatized her in adolescence. Thirteen years later
she was still determined to keep him as separate from her

life as he had chosen to become back then.

"Yes, but Sabrina," he was saying. "Even if you won't put the money to good use for yourself, you could at least invest it in your business. Your mother and I were talking about it last night, and—"

"Really? You've been communicating with your ex-wife? That's good of you."

There was a pause, and then he answered in a subdued tone. "You could go a little easier, you know." She was silent, and the distance between them crackled with faint voices and static. "This stubborn streak of yours can't be any good for your business," he began again.

"My business is *my* business," Sabrina said, drumming her fingers on her knee. "Okay? And really, I should be on my way to the office to take care of it."

"All right," he said quietly. "Give Lydia my best."

Sabrina ruminated on this conversation as she got dressed, putting a slouchy double-breasted vest of lambswool that buttoned at the hip over a knit skirt of matching navy and a pale blue silk crepe de chine blouse. So he was sending regards to Lydia now?

She remembered when Lydia, her mother's close friend from childhood, had offered Sabrina the partnership in her fledgling company back east, at the time of Sabrina's divorce. Her father had gotten wind of Sabrina's imminent move somehow, and had been virulently vocal in objecting to the whole enterprise. His sudden interest in it now was suspicious. Sabrina was used to, and didn't mind, the kindly surveillance that resulted from Lydia's friendship with her mom ("Lydia tells me you've been looking thin lately, dear—are you eating?" her mother might ask in a Sunday morning phone call), but the idea of her father being back in the fold, and privy to such details, disturbed her.

By eight-thirty she was done with her makeup and had shaken off the unsettling feelings the phone call had provoked. She was still on schedule, with plenty of time to pick up a newspaper and coffee en route to the crosstown bus—that is, if nothing unforeseen...

"All right, Van Dyke," she said, her hands on her hips, after a look beneath the dresser had confirmed her suspicions. "Let's have the earrings."

Carrie was still out, but one phone line was functional when Sabrina walked into the office. She called Lee Orloff immediately and left a message, as he wasn't in yet. She had just slit open the first of the stack of letters Lydia had handed her on her arrival when Lydia knocked on the wall between them.

"Phone for you," she called. "Pick up."

"Sabrina Hamilton," she said. "Hello."

"Good morning," said Drew Dalton. "How are things on your side of the block?"

At the first rumbling cadences of her caller's voice Sabrina identified him with embarrassing clarity as the man who had been in her dream. For a moment she was too disoriented to reply.

"Quiet? Off to a slow start?" he continued.

"No," she said, recovering. "Actually I'm quite busy." She glanced nervously out the window. He wasn't visible in the penthouse across the way.

"You never did tell me where you wanted to eat," he said. "And I'd like to make reservations. What time would be good for you?"

She nearly smiled at his sheer audacity, but kept her voice cool and even. "No time. We didn't make a date for tonight, Mr. Dalton."

"Well, that's terrible," he said blithely. "I've been looking forward to it. Don't tell me you're working late again?"

A metallic click on the line alerted her that another call was coming through. "Can you hold, please?" she asked, and then temporarily disconnected him. It was Carrie, her voice evidence of a badly stuffed nose, saying she would make it in after noon. Sabrina thanked her, then got back to Drew. "Mr. Dalton," she said, "I don't see any reason—"

"Get rid of that call-waiting," he interrupted. "You need a Comptrex-4 system—you know, one line that feeds into three additional numbers automatically?"

"It's already been ordered," she told him testily. "Perhaps you'd like to advise me on the color of my extension?"

"Well, you should get something that looks good against that stunning brown hair of yours," he mused, the husky resonance of his voice tickling her inner ear. "When *do* you let it down, Miss Hamilton?"

"None of your business," she said. "And unless it's something about business that you wish to discuss, I'd like—"

"Glad you reminded me. I had my secretary dig out some brochures on the Orange 805 Business System—that's the computer we use over here. I thought you might want to take a look at the information."

"I appreciate your concern," she said. "But there's really no need—"

"The Telestarter you mentioned won't do the trick," he said. "But why don't we discuss this over drinks? There's a place that's just opened up the block, on Sixty—"

"Mr. Dalton, for a man who prides himself on speed and efficiency, you're taking an awfully long time getting a very simple message. I'm not interested."

"Well, if you don't want to talk about computers, you can tell me about yourself. How would six o'clock be?"

Sabrina sighed. "N-o, no. No thanks," she repeated for emphasis. "Is that clear enough?"

"Well, let's see. My Friday night is free—"

"Forget it."

"You're not being very neighborly," was his mild reproach.

"You're not being very reasonable," she said. "I have to get back to work."

"All right then," he said breezily. "I'll call later."

"Don't bother," she said in a clipped tone, and hung up. She swiveled to face the window. Was it her imagination, or had a silhouetted figure just turned from the glass doors of the penthouse? "Go away!" she exclaimed to the window.

"Sabrina?" Lydia's voice floated from around the wall.

Sabrina rose from her desk and went into the other office. Lucy was standing stiffly by Lydia's desk in the larger room, diligently writing in a ledger. Lucy was a matronly, patrician woman whose scrupulously calculated balances were as perfect as her posture. When Sabrina entered, Lucy was nodding as she wrote, at Lydia's list of office supplies needed.

"More of those manila folders, a dozen boxes of paper clips, and reinforcements—"

"Shades," Sabrina said, sinking into the leather chair opposite Lydia.

Lydia raised her eyebrows.

"My window needs a shade," Sabrina said.

"We've already ordered those Levolor blinds," Lydia reminded her.

"I'll tack up a sheet," Sabrina muttered.

"And we're low on the cream-colored stationery," Lydia finished. "When Carrie comes in, have her call Whitson's with these orders. Maybe we should have moved right into their store instead of here," she added. "We've practically bought them out over the past month as it is." Lucy nodded, closed her ledger with a snap, and walked quickly from the room, her carriage erect. Lydia put out her cigarette and looked over her glasses at Sabrina. "What's with you?"

Sabrina told her, with some of the more discomfiting details glossed over, of her meeting Drew Dalton the day before. Lydia listened, amused, to her account of their argument. Then she leaned back in her Eames chair, tapping the eraser of a pencil against the edge of her desk.

"He has a point, of course," she mused.

"What do you mean?"

"Well, I have wondered if Evans Resources would be accused of sexist practices—when we've become well enough known to invite such attacks."

"That's ridiculous," said Sabrina. "You told me yourself you were starting this company to *combat* sexism. You saw that women speakers at other bureaus were being overshadowed by the men, not getting the same fees. You wanted to bring those awful 'spouse programs' out of the Dark Ages—and give the wives of executives attending conventions more to think about than flower arranging and fashion tips."

"But that doesn't mean we should be ruling out men entirely," Lydia replied. "Moss Affiliates has a men's division."

Moss Affiliates was their main competition in Manhattan, the only other bureau specializing in women speakers, and the larger, more established company.

"I know," Sabrina said. "We've talked this out before. I suppose we could use the publicity and prestige a Drew Dalton would give us," she admitted with a sigh. "But wouldn't it mean a lot more if we could enter the big leagues by getting an exclusive contract with, say, a Barbara Walters?"

"Of course it would," said Lydia, lighting up another cigarette. "But I think it's true that our women-only policy may be hurting us. Evans Resources needs to upgrade and expand. And if beginning a men's division will help..."

"I suppose it's inevitable," Sabrina agreed grudgingly.

"It could be that the time has come," Lydia said slowly. She turned in her chair to gaze out her window, which faced Drew's building. "This could be the offer we need to take. It certainly would start a new division off with a bang," she said, then turned back to Sabrina. "What's our Mr. Penthouse like?"

"A know-it-all. He's arrogant in the way men like him usually are... You know, too good-looking for their own good."

"Got under your skin a little, did he?" Lydia smiled as Sabrina glared at her. "I wouldn't mind being wined and dined at the likes of Dominique's on a regular basis—or sharing a modest nest like that," she added, indicating the window.

"But, of course, I'm a married woman," she continued, turning back to Sabrina. Sabrina didn't like the look in her senior partner's eye. At the moment she could have been standing in for Sabrina's mother.

"I've got a lot of mail to get through," Sabrina told her, and hurried back to her office. The phone was ringing as she reached her desk.

The morning continued to be busy. There were calls to and from clients and accounts, and mailings to go out. With the company's second-year expansion, and the move to a larger space, it was apparent that hiring an account executive was long overdue. Moderate success had increased the workload beyond the capabilities of their five-woman office. When Carrie came in, Lydia left for lunch, but Sabrina had too much on her hands to take a break.

Lydia had just left the office when Lee Orloff got back to her. Meeting planner for one of the largest business associations in the country, he was an acquaintance of Lydia's from her fund-raising days, and had taken a liking to Sabrina. She'd worked for months to find him the right speaker for an important convention on the West Coast, and would learn, now, how the woman—a former Commissioner of Consumer Affairs—had done. A good report might yield big opportunities for Evans.

"We loved her," Lee said heartily, after the usual amenities. "She was great for the spouse program, and we've really enjoyed working with you. You did everything beautifully." He sighed. "It's a shame you gals can't help me out of the jam I'm in now."

"What's that?"

"Well, you know, we've got our Man of the Year dinner at the St. Beaumont this weekend, Friday night? We were all set with the Secretary of State—and I just got the phone call this morning. He's canceled, and we're out a keynoter."

"That's terrible, Lee," she said, her mind racing. He was referring to a lavish sit-down dinner for 300 top executives at one of the most elegant ballrooms in the city. It was the kind of booking she'd give anything to get for one of their speakers. "Maybe I could book Vanessa Brown for you, or—"

"Wouldn't do, Sabrina. I hate to admit it, but it's a dyed-in-the-wool chauvinist organization we've got here. For a keynote speaker, they'll only take a man."

Sabrina cursed silently, her fingers drumming on her desktop. Then with a speed beyond rationality, an idea took shape, and the words were out of her mouth before she had time to regret them. "What if I could get you a man, Lee? Would you be interested in Drew Dalton?"

His answer was a whistle of admiration. "Interested? Honey, Dalton's book is sort of a management bible around here. Don't kid with me, now—since when do you represent male speakers? You got him on hand?"

"Would you be willing to spend twenty thousand plus?"

"Sabrina, in less than three days I've got three hundred C.E.O.'s from all over the country flying in to eat some filet mignon with a celebrity speaker. And at the moment I've got a big fat empty seat at the head of the dais. You get me Drew Dalton and you got the deal."

"Hold tight for a few minutes, Lee," she said. "I'll call you right back."

She hung up, dialed Information, and got the number of Dalton Enterprises on Sixty-seventh Street. A secretary with an exuberantly musical voice answered on the second ring. Sabrina gave her name and asked for Drew.

"What shall I say this is in reference to?"

Sabrina considered. "A date," she told the woman, and was put on hold.

A few minutes later Drew picked up. "I feel as though the sun has just burst through the clouds," he said. "I've put all my calls on hold and I'm ready to alert the chefs and wine stewards of Manhattan's finest cuisinaries. What's your pleasure, Miss Hamilton?"

"You mentioned Friday evening earlier," she said. "I take it you're free then?"

"Absolutely. I often stay in on weekend nights."

"So you have no other engagements?"

"Not a one."

Sabrina took a deep breath. "What would you say to a dinner at the St. Beaumont—a little steak, a little wine, and some talk—to the tune of fifteen thousand dollars?"

There was a pause. When he spoke again, Drew sounded less jubilant. "I see," he said wryly. "Something tells me we wouldn't be alone?"

"There'd be about three hundred other dinner guests, yes," she admitted. "The American Apparel Association is giving their Man of the Year award."

"Kind of short notice for an organization like that," he observed. "Who canceled?"

"The Secretary of State," she told him. "And now they won't settle for anyone less important than you. Aren't you flattered?"

"I'd be more flattered if this wasn't a business call," he said.

"Well?" she asked. "You made me an offer—a business offer—yesterday, and I'm taking you up on it. Obviously you weren't planning on being knee-deep in research and writing this Friday night, so—"

"So I have no excuse," he finished with a rueful chuckle. "I see your men's speaker division has sprung up rather quickly," he added.

"I can have a contract drawn up for you this afternoon," Sabrina said. "What do you say?"

He gave her a few moments of suspense. "All right."

"Thank you," Sabrina said, and it was heartfelt. "I see you work out of your home, so I'll have the contract delivered—"

"—by carrier pigeon?"

"—by messenger, before three o'clock. We provide all of our speakers with an information update—that's an organizational sheet with audience profile, dress code, everything you'll need to know. Is there anything specific you'll want in your contract that we should know about?"

"Yes, actually, there is one proviso—but I won't ask for it in writing. Your verbal agreement will do."

"Yes?"

"I want a dinner with you—a real one, no business involved. I pick the night, the time, and the place."

It was blackmail, pure and simple. Sabrina winced, then directed a frustrated look at the ceiling. "Okay," she said. "Fair is fair, I suppose."

"Good," he said. "I have an agent who handles these things. His name is Sandy O'Byrne, and you can reach him at 555-4576. I'll talk to him myself within the hour. Are we all set?"

"All set."

"Great," he said convivially. "By the way, I admire your taste in stockings. So long."

With a muttered oath Sabrina swung her feet off the chair by her desk and smoothed her skirt down over her thighs as she rose, angrily turning to the window. Drew's silhouette wasn't visible in any of the penthouse's windows across the street, but she paced to the corner of her room by the door and hovered there, out of range.

She supposed a dinner with the man wasn't too high a price to pay for landing such a plum engagement. As the echoes of his deep, sexy rumble of a voice reverberated in her ear, she pictured Drew Dalton as she'd first seen him—a delicious-looking specimen of magnetic masculinity, his devilish blue eyes seductively probing hers.

You might even enjoy yourself, whispered a wicked inner voice.

I have an important phone call to make, she reminded herself. As she dialed Lee Orloff to give him the good news,

Sabrina reflected that Lydia would probably be so pleased at this new development, she'd forget to be annoyed that Sabrina had acted so impulsively. Evans Speaker Resources was about to upgrade and expand—fast.

3

SABRINA PACED THE PLUSH, red-and-gold embroidered carpet of the St. Beaumont lobby. Ten minutes earlier, as the waiters inside had begun clearing the thirty oval tables for the elaborate dessert courses to come, she had left the ballroom and gone to a pay phone, acting on Sandy O'Byrne's specific instructions. Drew had chosen to skip the dinner itself, wanting only to be notified when dessert was being served. His limousine would then whisk him across town, his arrival timed to synchronize with the second round of coffee. "He likes to walk in, get his bearings, and then hit the podium," Sandy had informed her. "And make sure there's no press around before he speaks—they can get a few minutes with him afterward."

Drew's agent had turned out to be a tough cookie. Sandy O'Byrne went over every detail of the booking with her as if it were an armed robbery. He had started out openly distrustful and wary of working with a small company he'd never heard of, and a women's bureau as well. By exerting every ounce of her charm, and by paying careful attention to details, Sabrina had managed to win his grudging acceptance. But she'd been at the Beaumont since six that evening, personally overseeing everything, taking no chances. It wasn't just O'Byrne she wanted to impress. Sabrina was determined that Drew Dalton should have no opportunity to criticize her efficiency.

She checked her reflection in one of the lobby's floor-length wall mirrors. The pale beige crepe dress she wore was sheer and form-fitting, high-necked, with a tie that hung down her back. The material was snug around her torso but flared out at the hips. The absence of elaborate jewelry gave her outfit an elegant simplicity, she thought. She enjoyed being able to do business in a more feminine attire. Sabrina ran her fingers through her bangs and smoothed her hair, today combed back and worn loose over her shoulders, then turned to face the revolving doors at the hotel's main entrance. She could feel the adrenaline racing through her veins. Would they be late? Not very likely.

Sabrina had to smile at her own nervousness. She understood more than ever Lydia's reluctance to attend any of their bookings. "My nerves get frayed enough taking care of our clients from behind this desk," she'd told Sabrina, who had evinced surprise at her unwillingness to come to the St. Beaumont. "Besides, Dalton's your baby. You just give me a full report when the shouting's over."

"Excuse me—are you waiting for Drew Dalton?"

Sabrina tore her eyes away from the door. An attractive blonde in a stylish sequined pantsuit, with an incongruously staid black bag slung over her shoulder, was smiling expectantly at her.

"I'm Kay Cristy, from *Personality*," the woman went on, as Sabrina didn't immediately answer. "We've been working up a story on Drew, but we haven't managed to schedule an interview as yet. Are you expecting him here?"

She indicated the main entrance. Sabrina was familiar with the gossipy, soft-news weekly magazine the woman worked for. Who wasn't? It was as much an American staple by now as *TV Guide*. But remembering O'Byrne's edict about the press, Sabrina avoided a direct answer.

"Mr. Dalton's agent, Mr. O'Byrne, should be along here shortly," she told the woman. "I think Mr. Dalton's expected to talk to the press after his speech. Are you going to hear it?"

"I'll be there," the woman said vaguely, flashing her automatic smile again. "Well, look—" She rummaged in her bag and produced a card. "If you do see Dalton before I have an opportunity to, would you give him this? He's been a difficult man to get in touch with."

"All right," Sabrina said, taking it.

"Are you with Harry Sprint?"

Sabrina shook her head. Sprint's speaker bureau was one of the largest in the country, and the top of the line in New York. "No," she told the woman, with a trace of pride. "Evans Speaker Resources."

Though Sabrina doubted she'd heard of them, Kay Cristy nodded as if she recognized the name, then headed for the ballroom, all sparkles. When Sabrina turned back to the door, a short, stocky man in a dark suit, with thinning hair and aviator glasses, was leading Drew Dalton into the lobby. Undoubtedly Sandy O'Byrne. She stepped forward to greet him, but her eyes were automatically drawn to Drew. Her heart did a quick, unaccountable flip-flop as his gaze met hers, and his radiantly handsome features lit up in a smile of recognition.

She hadn't spoken to Drew since their phone conversation Tuesday; when she'd called earlier, a woman had answered and taken her message about the approach of dessert. Sabrina felt a twinge of annoyance at the increased beating of her pulse as she came to meet him. What was the matter with her?

"Miss Hamilton?" The smaller man's handshake was brisk and firm. "You've met Drew, of course?"

"Hello," he said simply. He gave her a smile that seemed to intimate they were sharing some private joke. She found herself smiling back, then halted in mid-grin, glancing at Sandy O'Byrne's impassive face. She wondered how many details of her initial meeting with Drew he'd told the agent.

"It's this way, gentlemen," Sabrina said in her most businesslike tone, and led them across the hushed, ornate lobby to the ballroom's entrance. John Dysinger, a perennially worried-looking man who was Lee Orloff's assistant, met them just outside the door. Sabrina held a brief whispered conference with him, then returned to Sandy and Drew.

"They'll be ready for Drew in about five minutes," Sabrina told the agent, then turned to Drew. "If you'd like to go in and get a feel of the audience, there's a chair for you at the table closest to the dais."

Drew nodded. As he passed Sabrina going in, he leaned forward slightly, his face grazing her hair. "Umm," he murmured by her ear. "Smells wonderful, too." Sabrina could only stand there, her lips clamped shut, as he gave her a barely perceptible wink. Then he entered the ballroom with Dysinger.

Sandy turned to her, indicating the little table by the entrance to the ballroom that had been set up to hold complimentary copies of Drew's book. "How'd you come by those?" He pointed at the small pile of paperbacks.

"Bookvendors was late with the shipment of Drew's books," she explained. "But I managed to wrangle two hundred and fifty advance copies of the paperback version out of the publisher."

"Nice," said O'Byrne. "The paperbacks aren't in the stores yet." He nodded, his lips pursed. Sabrina could sense a subtle deference in his usually cucumber-cool manner. "Is Ms. Evans here as well?"

"I'm sorry, she had a prior engagement that she couldn't cancel."

He nodded again and adjusted his glasses. "Well, so far so good," he noted. "The two of you have done a good job."

"Thank you."

"Before we go in—" He paused at the door. "Have you got the check?"

Sabrina paled. "The check?" she repeated.

Sandy O'Byrne frowned. "I told Ms. Evans in our first conversation that Drew expects his payment on the night of the engagement."

Sabrina cleared her throat, which had suddenly gone quite dry. "We always pay our clients within twenty-four hours," she explained. "I had been planning to send the check over by messenger first thing in the morning." She added mentally, *after I strangle my boss for leaving this one salient detail out of her instructions.*

O'Byrne shook his head, opening the door for her. "After you," he muttered.

They stood together just inside the entrance. The cavernous oval room buzzed with the talk of businessmen in black tie, digesting their ice cream bombes beneath tiered chandeliers. A pianist tinkled soothingly at the far end of the room, his white grand piano gilt-edged to match the wainscotting.

"There's Drew," O'Byrne murmured at her ear. She followed his gaze to one of the tables a few yards away. He was talking to an executive's wife, the highlights of his hair gleaming in the soft rose light. "There's an empty seat next to him," O'Byrne went on with studied casualness. "Why don't you just go on over there and tell Drew that you haven't got his check. I think he'd be interested in knowing that."

"Now?" Sabrina asked.

"Now," he replied firmly.

The air in the room felt decidedly chillier as she crossed

the parquet floor. Steeling herself, Sabrina slipped into the chair next to Drew. She examined his profile as he talked to his companion. She sensed he had made an immediate conquest of the older woman. Would he be as charming when Sabrina gave him her bit of news? Before she had a chance to formulate a way into broaching the subject, Drew had turned to her. His glittering eyes moved quickly over her face, frankly appraising her features, then coming to a rest on her lustrous hair.

"You've made my evening," he said, and before she could stop him, he was running his hand through the silky tresses. She moved away, conscious that the gentle touch of his fingers gliding by her face had been electrically titillating.

"Drew, there's something I have to tell you," she began, smoothing her hair back behind her ears nervously.

"It's not a fall, is it? A wig? I don't believe you."

She sighed at the mock alarm on his face, and shook her head. "Drew..." She paused, stalling. "Has everything been all right so far? Everything satisfactory?"

He nodded. "I'm especially enjoying the added dividend of seeing you in that dress," he said, his eyes roaming appreciatively over her outfit.

"The travel arrangements? No problem?"

Drew examined her face. "You're about to tell me that there *is* a problem," he observed.

Sabrina looked him straight in the eye. "I don't have your check," she said quietly. "There was a mix-up in communications. We'd been planning to messenger it over to you tomorrow morning."

Only the hint of a raised eyebrow hinted at any reaction on Drew's face. He continued to hold her gaze for a long, silent moment. Then he looked down, glancing at his watch.

"Well, it's not too late to catch a movie. A few opened this week that I'm curious to see."

"You wouldn't," she gasped.

"Of course I wouldn't," he said mildly. "That would be unprofessional."

The not-so-subtle barb in his last words was stinging in her ears as Drew rose, having sensed John Dysinger hovering around his chair. The lights above them had dimmed. As the flush in her cheeks slowly subsided and her pulse returned to normal, Sabrina watched Drew take his place on the dais and listened to the association's chairman give a brief introductory speech. A number of words to describe Drew came to her mind, but even the most insulting seemed too tame.

As the applause died down Drew adjusted his microphone at the raised podium, his eyes quickly scanning the sea of faces. Again she had to remind herself that the man wasn't really tall; he just seemed to be. He automatically commanded the attention of even the waiters. A few paused at the door leading off to the kitchen, trays in hand, to listen to the opening of Drew's speech.

"You're here tonight to honor your Man of the Year," he began. "And I'm here to offer you the theory that to become a Man of the Year, one first has to be a man of the moment."

His deep, resonant voice was ideal for public speaking, Sabrina noted. Even some of the most prominent authors on the circuit were not natural orators, but Drew definitely had "it"—and his audience, from his first words.

"I dislike long-winded speeches myself," he went on. "But for once I'll take more than one minute"—he paused as chuckles of recognition swept the room—"to talk about the crucial seconds in every working day that can make the difference between break-even mediocrity and record-breaking success."

Politely but firmly Sabrina maneuvered into position amid the guests gathered around Drew. Sandy O'Byrne had instructed her to pull the speaker out of this still-unthinning

crowd, and give him safe passageway through the lobby.
She attempted to catch Drew's eye over the many books
held open for autographing. She grudgingly admired his
staying power. Most speakers would spend a cursory few
minutes talking to members of the audience after a speech,
and some would leave directly. But Drew had been at his
table for nearly a half hour.

Sabrina deftly elbowed her way to his side and bent to
whisper in his ear as he signed another book. "Sandy wants
me to get you out of here," she told him. "He's gone to get
the limo driver."

Drew nodded, said a few words to the tuxedo-clad man
whose book he'd just signed, and rose. With Sabrina helping
to shield him from the onslaught of proffered hands, he
extricated himself. In a few moments they were at the door
to the lobby.

"Thanks," he said, opening the door for her. "I really
needed to come up for air."

As they stepped into the lobby Sabrina saw Kay Cristy
headed toward them. Drew halted as she did.

"Uh-oh," he muttered. "Miss Personality."

"You know her?"

"She's been after me for an interview all week." He
sighed. "Practically camped on my doorstep. Putting her
off again would be bad politics, but I'm not in the mood
for this at all right now..." Drew glanced to their side.
"Here," he said, taking Sabrina by the arm. "Let's avoid
the issue altogether."

Before Sabrina could protest he was whisking her through
the doors of the hotel's smaller ballroom, adjacent to the
main one. Soft swing music from the forties filled the dimly
lit room. A small orchestra of men in white tuxedos played
on a circular bandstand, and couples danced beneath a glittering ball. Drew took her by the hand and headed for the
long, gleaming black bar.

"She's following us in," Sabrina said, having glanced

over her shoulder in mid-flight. She tried to remove her hand from his, but he held it, and drew her even closer. "What are you—" she began. With a gentlemanly little bow, Drew swung her out onto the dance floor.

It had all happened so quickly that she was breathless as his arms slid around her. His hands, moving smoothly to grasp her at the shoulder and the small of her back, held her gently but firmly in place. Struggling was useless. She couldn't help but rest her hands on his shoulders. For the first time in as long as she could remember, a man had her completely in his control. A shiver shook her from head to foot and she realized, shocked, that she really didn't want to struggle loose.

"I think we'll be safe here," Drew murmured, glancing around her at the other couples on the floor.

You may be safe, she groaned inwardly. Speak for yourself! She looked up at the handsome, smiling face only inches from her own, and her stomach seemed to plummet. His eyes gazed steadily into hers. The powerful, determinedly seductive force of their velvet depths seemed to pull from deep inside her a sensual, wanton desire long hidden. She couldn't help but be aware of her breasts pressing against the firmness of his chest, couldn't shut out the deliciously insinuating movement of his firm thighs against her own. A chorus of protesting voices were blathering alarm in her woozy head, but, nonetheless, her arms settled into place around his shoulders. She'd never reacted to a man this way before, not Wayne, not anyone. It was crazy.

And it was heavenly. As the slow dreamy music of the gently cooing horns worked its insidiously romantic spell, Sabrina found herself relaxing under the subtle pressure of Drew's warm hands on her back. Her body was melding to his. He was holding her closer in his arms now, and she could feel the feathery touch of his lips by her ear.

She told herself she'd allowed herself this indulgence, this extreme breach of better judgment, long enough, and it was time to put some distance between her trembling body and this predatory hunk of masculinity. She didn't, though. She danced.

"I could do this all night long," Drew said. "You dance beautifully."

"Shouldn't we be getting you out of here?" She might as well have been addressing herself.

"I can't think of any other place I'd rather be," he answered.

I can't think, period. Her heart beat in time with his as they swayed under the soft lights. When she turned her head slightly, her parted lips brushed his cheek. She tasted the faint, pungent salty sweetness of his skin, and inhaled his subtle but virile masculine scent. She forced herself to keep her eyes open as dizziness threatened to overtake her. This isn't happening. I'm not here; it's someone else who's melting into a pool of liquid sensuality.

But it was, undeniably, her hand that moved slowly on the back of his neck, her fingers gliding through his soft, thick hair. It was her hips that seemed to fuse against his as the music rose; her breasts whose tips swelled to hardness as they pressed against his chest. Drew was lightly nuzzling her neck, his warm lips tickling the lobe of her ear, sending tremors of delectable exhilaration coursing through her.

And then, before she practically swooned against his lithe, supple body, the song ended. Couples around them were applauding politely, and though she was still in Drew's embrace, she had room to breathe again. Grateful for the reprieve, and gathering her wits again, Sabrina slid her hands across his shoulders and rested them against his chest.

"Is the coast clear?" she asked him, peering into the smoky light around the bar.

He squinted, staring over her shoulder. Then suddenly he grasped her chin with his hand. "Kiss me," he commanded softly.

"What?"

"Kiss me," he repeated urgently.

"But—"

She could see her own startled image reflected in his turquoise eyes. She assumed by his actions that Kay Cristy was approaching them, and he wanted help in a last ruse to avoid the woman. As Sabrina felt his hand close around the nape of her neck, holding her still, her lips automatically parted, even as she willed them to close. With a tiny shudder of anticipation she tilted her face up to meet his.

At the first touch of his lips on hers, the last vestiges of rational thought were swept away. She was filled with the swirling sensations of his mouth and tongue teasing hers as the kiss became more heated. His tongue was gliding between her lips, then sliding deep into her mouth to touch her tongue. A voluptuous warmth blossomed in her body and she pressed her lips to his, harder, a fiery need uncoiling to meet his insistent demands. No longer a prisoner in his grasp but an accomplice, she arched her back, her palms tightening on his shoulders as their tongues meshed.

The brisk booming of a snare drum's downbeat brought her abruptly back to earth. The band was starting an up-tempo number. Sabrina blinked open her eyes and stared dazedly into Drew's. He was looking at her with undisguised satisfaction. Something about the hint of a smile that hovered about the edges of his mouth set off a rapid succession of emotions in her. She was mortified, outraged, and ultimately furious with herself in an instant.

You idiot! How could you have let this smug, arrogant lug hold you like that and turn you into a quivering mass of Jell-O with a single kiss? And good God, he's a client, besides!

"Fantastic," he said, a strange gleam in his eye. She removed herself from his grip before he could make any further attempt to completely unhinge her.

"Was that really necessary?" she asked.

"Absolutely." He smiled.

"Is she gone?"

"Gone? Who?" He looked at her blankly. "Oh, that woman

from the magazine," he said. "Yes, she left as soon as we began to dance."

If she had been furious with herself a moment earlier, it was now he who received the full force of her look of scathing rage. "You snake," she began. "Of all the low-down—"

"You enjoyed it, didn't you?" he said innocently.

"—dirty tricks I've ever—"

"You did."

"—had the misfortune to suffer at the hands—"

"I did, too."

"—of the apelike male population of this godforsaken city—"

"Shall we have a drink?"

Sabrina closed her mouth and merely stared.

"What would you like?" he asked.

"As of now, Mr. Dalton, you're no longer my responsibility," she said, forcibly keeping her voice low and even. "I think I've done more than enough for you this evening as it is. Your limousine and your probably by-now-impatient manager are outside the main entrance. So if you'll excuse me—"

"Leaving? I'll give you a lift home."

"No," she said with a tight-lipped smile. "You won't."

She turned quickly on her heel and strode from the dance floor. Get that check out to him first thing in the morning, she told herself as she went to collect her coat. Tell Lydia that from now on, any dealings with Drew Dalton would be Lydia's job, not hers. Then paint the damn window over, or nail the new blinds shut. Maybe she'd never have to see hide or hair of him again. If any dates came up for male speakers—

Dates. Oh, no.

Sabrina stood stock-still a moment near the revolving doors. He couldn't—he wouldn't—

He would.

4

VAN DYKE KNEW something was up. He'd been following Sabrina around the apartment as she dressed, his meowing like a running commentary as she tried on one outfit and then another. As eight o'clock approached, and Sabrina began to pick up speed, the cat eventually lay down in the center of the floor, head in his paws, only his eyes keeping up with her movements.

To ride the line between business and leisure she'd ultimately opted for a light-gray linen dress that was cut long and narrow, with deep dolman sleeves and a neckline that didn't plunge. The black and silver belt she added suggested simple silver bangle bracelets on one arm and black onyx earrings—one of the few gifts from Wayne she kept in use. Her appearance, as she appraised it in the mirror, was casually dressy, and not overtly seductive. Her hair, after a long inward debate, had ended up loose and down—not to please the overattentive Mr. Dalton, but because... Because she felt like it.

Sabrina paced a circle around Van Dyke, enumerating a short mental list of do's and don't's for herself as the hour hand on her wall clock nudged the eight. Do keep the conversation as superficial as possible. Don't maintain eye contact for longer than split-second intervals. Do assure the gentleman your business is doing just fine without his help, thank you. And don't—absolutely do not—dance with Drew Dalton.

The buzzer sounded. She jumped. Van Dyke gave a perfunctory yelp and Sabrina shushed him. She pressed the intercom. "Hello?"

"Hi, there. I'm double-parked—"

"I'll be right down," she told him, and let go of the little button.

She got her coat and added a long woolen scarf; it was already getting cold in mid-October. As she locked up the apartment and headed for the elevator, Sabrina wondered what sort of car Drew would be driving. He could probably afford a Mercedes. A Bentley or the likes of it struck her as too ostentatious for him... Wayne had driven a Jaguar. The car had made him feel racier, more young at heart than he really was.

Sabrina sighed. Why had Wayne been on her mind so much recently? She stepped into the elevator. Yes, of course, Drew did remind her of her ex-husband superficially. Both men were self-assured to a point of arrogance, they were moneyed, and powerful, and... There the resemblance ended. Wayne, she mused, had ultimately been rather stodgy, a cold fish. But Drew was anything but cold. That was what she found most intimidating about him, wasn't it? The sense she had that beneath the cool exterior was an animallike heat just barely held in check—this was the quality that required keeping him at arm's length.

Drew had kept his distance for a few days after the

Beaumont engagement. She'd welcomed the temporary reprieve as she'd welcomed the arrival of her Levolor blinds.
When a few days passed without any word—Sandy O'Byrne
had called in to thank them for the check's prompt arrival
and a job well done—Sabrina began to think that Drew had
forgotten about his oral addition to their contract. But no,
he called bright and early one morning, apologizing for
having been out of touch. As if she'd been waiting to hear
from him! He commended her on her choice of blinds and
gave her the specifications of their date to come: The Riverview Restaurant, a posh and romantic place that faced the
Manhattan skyline from across the river in Brooklyn, and
thus, the necessity of his picking her up in his car. He neatly
maneuvered his way through her prepared obstacle course
of nights she was unavailable (she actually had only one
date scheduled for the upcoming week, but was not about
to make things easy for him) and caught her off-guard by
proposing (since next week seemed so busy) that they go
out the following night. Feeling she might as well get it
over with, Sabrina had acquiesced.

Now, here she was, stepping out into the brisk night air,
her gentleman suitor holding open the door of a—what?
Sabrina paused, staring at the futuristic contraption that
hugged the pavement in front of her building. It looked
more like a mini-spaceship from a sci-fi flick than an au-
tomobile. The sleek, streamlined vehicle was all black and
chrome, the wide, nearly wraparound windshield tinted a
dark opaque gray.

Drew greeted her with a smile and a chivalrous bow.
Sabrina hesitated at the door of the car, built so low to the
ground, she fantasized one had to be craned into it through
the silver roof.

"Are we going to Brooklyn or another galaxy?" she asked
dryly.

"Possibly both," he answered, shrugging. "It's supremely comfortable," he assured her. "You'll see once
you're inside the seats have been designed to fit the contours

of the average human body for maximum efficiency and relaxation. Of course, for above-average bodies, one can make adjustments," he added, poker-faced.

Sabrina glared at him briefly, then bent down, hunched herself over, and slid into the car with as much ladylike élan as she could manage. He shut the door firmly behind her. As Sabrina stretched out her legs she had to admit the firm but plushly upholstered seat was comfortable and the interior not as cramped as it would seem. A flashing light with a computer-printed message on the panel in front politely requested that she fasten her seat belt.

As Drew got in beside her she noted that the entire instrument panel appeared to be computerized. Basically flat, with a myriad of little, touch-sensitive buttons, it put her in mind of that preposterous car on television that talked like a humanized robot. Drew turned the ignition and the motor purred to life. The tiny flashing lights on the space-age dashboard and the ultra-modern interior made an incongruous contrast with the music that was gently piping from unseen speakers: Peruvian folk music, flutes played by Indians. She recognized it immediately as an album she owned and had long treasured.

"I thought I was one of the only people in New York City who listened to South American folk music," she said, unable to keep the pleased surprise out of her voice.

"Really? 'La Flute Indienne.' You know it?" She nodded. "I collect the stuff," he said, easing the sleek machine into traffic. "I've got the whole Folkways series on tape—you're welcome to come by and peruse it anytime."

Sabrina nodded again, the lilting, sweet-sad haunting flutes of the jungle conjuring up images of lush greenery and deep-blue rivers in her mind as the cityscape of sky-scrapers glinted by outside her window. She glanced at Drew, imagining for a moment that he sported loincloth and lionskin rather than the charcoal-gray pinstripe suit. That was what he reminded her of, she realized—a leonine, lordly savage who had metamorphosed into a well-groomed predator of the concrete jungle.

Hold it right there, she commanded herself. Put the fantasy life on ice. The one point worth remembering is that the man is dangerous —no doubt he eats susceptible females for breakfast and pays obeisance to only one goddess: Success. She turned her attention to the panel in front of her again.

"Does this thing do windows?" she asked.

Drew chuckled. "Just about everything but. It's a DXL-two—a model a friend of mine designed. It's not on the market as yet. He wanted me to test-drive it for city use. The car's actually built to raise dust on the highways. Forcing this machine to sit in metropolitan traffic is like using a Concorde to fly from here to Buffalo."

"What do you usually drive then?"

"I've got an old Volvo. But it's in the shop. And I'm always curious to check out the latest advance in technology. It pays to get a look at what's coming—saves a lot of time scrambling to catch up when your competition's already a step ahead." He glanced sideways at Sabrina. "I imagine that's what you're up against now."

"What do you mean?" she said, stiffening.

"Well, I imagine if your men's division is just getting off the ground, you and Lydia must be working overtime."

"We're handling it," she said coolly.

Drew glanced at her, a smile playing at the corners of his mouth. He seemed about to ask another question, then thought better of it and merely nodded. Perhaps he sensed that she was poised, ready to do battle if he challenged her business expertise.

Sabrina returned her attention to the road, and the silhouetted skyline of lower Manhattan. The moon was full, a pale yellow oval punctured at its bottom by the black spires of old Wall Street buildings, their colonial domes and steeples dwarfed now by modern metal edifices twice their size. And then the moon was abruptly eclipsed by the World Trade Center's twin towers, looming above her to the right. The now barely perceptible tinting of the windshield seemed to render every glinting angle of the silver superstructure unnaturally sharp.

"This is my favorite part of the city," Drew mused aloud. "It's where everything began. When your office and my home were only meadows and forest, the center, the city's pulse was down here. In many ways it still is."

She'd never thought about such things—the infancy of New York City. To her it had been a nexus of power and energy sprung full-grown from an island of concrete. But as they passed an obviously centuries-old church flanked by narrow, twisting streets whose cobblestones, she realized, had only recently been repaved, a glimmer of the city's history revealed itself.

"Did you grow up here?" she asked Drew.

He shook his head. "I'm from Danbury, Connecticut," he told her. "But as soon as I got my M.B.A. I gravitated to the city. The atmosphere suits me here, I guess. I thrive on it." They were going up the ramp to the Brooklyn Bridge now, the pavement rumbling beneath them, the water below gleaming in the moonlight. "You're not from here, are you?"

"Up until a year or so ago I was living in San Francisco," she told him.

Drew nodded. "Nice place to visit."

"Too tame for you, I suppose," she said, bristling.

Drew shrugged. "It's a beautiful city," he said. "But it's always struck me as a little island floating off the coast of the world. A good spot to vacation—to retire to, perhaps."

A surge of her old San Francisco chauvinism overcame her. "I'm sure it seems ridiculously provincial to you," she began. "But you know, for us simple-minded folks, having clean air to breathe, beautiful weather, the best seafood in America—"

"—and the occasional earthquake, makes it all worthwhile. I know," he finished. "I don't mean to knock your hometown," he added mildly.

"It's not my hometown," she muttered. "I grew up in Los Angeles."

"Ah," he said, and then, obviously searching for something more complimentary to say, offered, "Great beaches."

"It's not even a city," she said crossly. "It's a glitzy overgrown suburb with no redeeming factors whatsoever. I got out of *there* as soon as *I* graduated college. So you don't have to be patronizing about it."

In the silence that followed Sabrina noted that the evening was off to a fine start. Drew Dalton appeared to have the knack of rubbing her the wrong way whenever she spent more than two consecutive minutes in his company. They were over the bridge now, and turning down a winding side street that led to the water. Drew seemed absorbed in driving, and unperturbed by the friction between them.

"I hope you're not completely determined to have a bad time with me tonight," he said quietly as they pulled into the parking lot of the Riverview. "Because this really is a special place."

The restaurant was a long, one-story building set right on the water's edge, nestled on the dock just below the soaring buttresses of the bridge. Beyond it the island of Manhattan glittered in all of its nighttime splendor across the silver expanse of water. The panorama was so picture-postcard perfect that Sabrina was stunned into wide-eyed admiration. "Why, it's . . . beautiful, Drew," she exclaimed. "I've never seen the city from here before."

"I thought you might like it," he said smoothly, unbuckling his seat belt. An attendant dressed in a smart, cruise-shiplike uniform of white and navy was opening the door for her. He peered into the recesses of the futuristic car as he helped Sabrina out, unable to disguise his fascination.

"Key in the ignition, sir?" he asked Drew, who was coming around to take Sabrina's arm.

"That's right," Drew told him. "Just don't take it into hyperspace." He left the attendant rather cautiously approaching the driver's seat. A doorman opened the restaurant's porthole-windowed door for them. Sabrina found that Drew's casual, gentlemanly guidance was doing strange things to her sense of equilibrium. His light touch on her arm created a tingling sensation there that she was too aware of. She realized, as Drew effortlessly attracted the undivided attention of the maître d', that walking at Drew's side induced in her an odd, suspended feeling, and that a great deal of her energy was being devoted to blocking out his all-too-physically palpable presence.

Her eyes roved over the beautifully appointed interior of the restaurant as the maître d' consulted his reservation list. One wall boasted a room-length picture window. Small tables covered with white tablecloths were bathed in the soft rose glow of nautically styled lamps that lined the spectacular view from one end to the other. The wood-paneling, with its porthole motif, continued the shipboard concept, and there was the subtle illusion that one was, in fact, in the splendiferous and genteel main dining room of some luxury ocean liner of a bygone age.

Once more Drew's hand was at her elbow. The graciously smiling maître d' led her to a table in the farthest corner of the room, a vantage point from which one could command a view of the entire place as well as directly overlook the water and the glittering lights of New York City across the river. One thing she could say for Drew Dalton—he had an innate sense of dramatic extravagance, whether it be the stunning modernity of his abode and car or this elegantly old-world eatery.

"Most of what you see here was originally on board the *Isabella II*," Drew informed her, following her gaze around the room. "It was one of the last of the big liners that made regular trips abroad between the wars. It was damaged in dock during the air raids in Britain, and the owners here bought up most of the dining room accoutrements at auction some years back. Makes for an interesting atmosphere, don't you think?"

Sabrina nodded. A wine steward was handing Drew a leatherbound wine list. He perused it a moment, then looked up at Sabrina.

"I suppose you'd like something dry?" he asked.

"As opposed to something sweet?" she returned, bristling.

"How about something in between?" he suggested.

"Fine," she said. Drew motioned the steward over and ordered a bottle of a French Cabernet wine with a vintage nearly as old as she was. Sabrina felt her hackles rising. She wished she could just relax and enjoy this rare instance of being pampered in high style, but something in her rebelled at the indulgence of it all, at men with money who flaunted it automatically, as her father always had, as Wayne . . .

"I'm sorry, perhaps you would have preferred a white wine? Or a soda?" Drew was looking at her quizzically. Sabrina realized she was glaring at the wine steward's retreating back. She quickly composed her features, giving Drew a patently friendly smile.

"No, I like red."

"I was beginning to think you had something against alcoholic beverages," he said. "You've been turning down invitations to drink with me ever since we met."

Sabrina shrugged. "So," she said, looking around her, "is this where the elite meet?"

"I wouldn't know."

"Don't you come here often?"

"I've only been here once before," he said. He looked at her, his brow furrowing. "Maybe you were in the mood for a more informal place. I noticed a number of Greek diners in your neighborhood. But I thought a date with a woman as lovely as you warranted an out-of-the-ordinary environment. I'm sorry if it's not to your taste."

"No," she said, flushing. "I'm sorry . . . It's really quite nice." She looked down at the tablecloth, embarrassed that he was reading her discomfort so easily. Their waiter was pouring wine. When he'd departed she looked up again.

"Here's to a long-standing relationship," Drew said, raising his glass in a toast.

She looked at him, momentarily startled. "A business relationship, you mean," she said, recovering.

"That'll do for this toast," he answered, smiling, and then added as she sipped the wine, "Don't you have any other kinds?"

Sabrina nearly choked on the delicious, richly pungent wine. "Excuse me?" she managed.

"Sabrina," Drew said, looking at her fondly as he leaned back in his chair, wineglass in hand. She tried to blink against the soft, seductive current radiating from his clear blue eyes. "Is it all men that you want nothing to do with? Or just me?"

Sabrina resisted an impulse to pitch the entire table over into his lap. Instead, she took another sip of wine and leaned back in her chair. "Just men like you," she answered evenly.

"But you barely know me," he objected.

"Let's keep it that way," she suggested.

Drew grinned. Lord, that disarming smile of his! She felt suddenly that they were friendly accomplices in some hugely enjoyable game. Sabrina looked away, out the window, where a shadowy barge strung with little Christmaslike lights slowly slid by beneath the bridge.

"There must have been some man in particular," Drew noted, "who's been serving as the role model." He leaned toward her. "Tell me. Who's the man who makes you assume that a man like me might be a man like him?"

"Come again?" She addressed his forehead (Avoid eye contact. That particular item from her mental list blipped in neon).

"Define your terms," Drew said dryly. "We'll start with that—what are the characteristics of a man like me?"

"Arrogance," she supplied promptly, her gaze shifting

now to meet his squarely. "Self-assurance to the point of obnoxiousness. A drive for success and status that overrides all other drives ... except one, which usually goes hand-in-hand with a perception of women as conquests, to be won and then kept in their places."

"Not the most likeable sort," he commented good-naturedly. "And that's how you see me?"

"So far," she admitted.

"Ah," he said, his eyes gleaming in the soft rose light. "Then at least you'll allow that there might be more to me than what you've seen."

Sabrina shrugged. His implacability in the face of her pointed attack on his character was unnerving. With Wayne such provocatively insulting remarks would have resulted in an out-and-out fight.

"The rest of me might be worth knowing," he said.

She stared at him. Had there been any deliberate sexual innuendo in his remark? Or was it her own imp of the perverse that conjured up an image in her mind of Drew's lithe, masculine physique minus his impeccably pressed suit and shirt? Sabrina looked away again, confused by the insidious tickle of arousal she felt at the image of an unclothed Drew. Perhaps she was doomed to be pathologically attracted to men she should by all rights despise. Perhaps it was time to slow down her wine intake.

"I'm sure you're all heart," she said caustically. "You give a good portion of your earnings to tax-deductible charities and you probably help little old ladies cross the street. You just *seem* like a profit-hungry powermonger, but you're really a sweet, sensitive guy."

Surely that had gotten a rise out of him. But no, he looked perfectly at ease, even amused. He cocked his head slightly, and the little streak of silver in his slightly disheveled hair glinted. "And you just *seem* like an overcompetitive, emotionally repressed man-hater, but you're actually just a pussycat," he suggested.

The foul-mouthed invective that was coming to her lips

was halted only by the appearance of the waiter at Sabrina's side. "Are you ready to order, miss?"

Sabrina clamped her mouth shut and glared at the menu. Well, she might as well get the most out of the meal. If Drew was cavalierly ordering hundred-dollar bottles of wine, she'd order the filet mignon.

She did. Drew ordered a salmon steak. When the waiter had departed, she met Drew's eyes again.

"I suppose I asked for that less than kindly description," she said stiffly. "But I guess neither of us deserves being stereotyped."

"No," he said simply. Drew leaned forward and his hand covered hers before she could move it away. "You're a beautiful woman, Sabrina," he said softly, his eyes gazing steadily into hers. "I have a feeling you're beautiful through and through . . . My feelings about people are usually on the mark. And I have a hunch that somebody must have hurt you pretty deeply to make you as defensive as you're being now. You don't have to be that way with me. I wish you wouldn't be."

With Drew's hand on hers, and the gentle, sympathetic current of understanding that emanated from his eyes, the defenses he was speaking of were hard to keep up. And he was right. The pain she'd felt from the divorce, the rejection and hopelessness she'd experienced, she had turned into a shield. She wasn't giving Drew a chance, perhaps precisely because she knew he had the power to invoke feelings in her that she didn't want to feel. But at the moment his perceptiveness seemed more friendly than antagonistic, his power more a comfort than a frightening challenge.

She stared at his hand on hers, feeling the warmth, the soft smoothness of his skin.

"What are you thinking?" he asked softly.

"You're right," she said, and, marshaling her strength, slowly drew her hand from under his. "You do have accurate hunches."

"You were married?"

"Briefly," she said, and took another sip of wine.

"But long enough to have acquired some scars," he observed shrewdly.

Sabrina nodded. Relieved of the tension the physical contact with Drew created, and avoiding his all-too-piercing gaze, she was regaining her balance, and the veil of objectivity she liked to cloak her marriage in descended once again. "I'm sure it's a common story," she said, affecting carelessness. "We—Wayne and I—didn't know each other very well before we got married. We made a lot of promises to each other along with the vows, and some of the more important ones were hard to keep."

"Such as?"

She sighed. "To love and honor is one thing. To obey..." She spread her palms in the air in a gesture of resignation. "Wayne was a lawyer on his way to becoming a partner in a successful firm, one of San Francisco's largest. When we met I was a fledgling journalist. I told him I wanted to get a job, and he didn't seem to have any objection to a two-career household. At first."

"Until you actually got one."

"That's right. A friend of mine had been an assistant editor at *The Coast Review*. That's a literary magazine out there, I doubt you—"

"I'm familiar with it," he said. "I like the caricatures that illustrate the articles. That artist—what's his name?"

"David Smithers," she said, surprised and flattered. "I was the one who got him to stay on as a staffer when the ownership changed hands."

Drew gave her an appreciative smile. "Go on."

"Oh. Anyway"—she paused, nodding a thanks as Drew refilled her glass—"when I started working, a few months after the honeymoon, things began to get tense. I enjoyed editing. I liked being in an office. *I* didn't feel competitive, honestly. Wayne was making over twice my salary, anyway—"

"But he felt you were."

"He wanted a housewife, to put it bluntly. And..." She traced the rim of her glass with her forefinger. She was glossing over a lot of things. But why delve deeper? She wasn't about to go into the more personal—and more painful—aspects of the friction that had developed between them with alarming speed and intensity. She wasn't going to recount or relive how inadequate Wayne had made her feel as a wife.

"And he wanted a family?"

"You're batting a thousand, Mr. Dalton," she said.

"You're awfully formal, Miss Hamilton." His tone was gently chiding.

"Sorry." She smiled in spite of herself. His annoyingly attractive looks and manner certainly did make maintaining her distance difficult. There was a quality in the man, a certain openness, that made her feel like pouring out the whole story. He was watching her with a definitely interested and intent look on his face, a face softened by the caring she saw there. It was a look that Wayne had had once, early in their courtship. But it had faded once she was his. The bitterness of the memory brought her up short.

"It's not all that interesting," she said abruptly. "I wasn't ready to have children. He was. We fought. It ended."

"Maybe sometime you'll tell me the more interesting story," he said.

"Meaning?"

"I mean all the stuff you left out."

She gave him a polite, tightlipped smile. "Maybe. But you haven't told me a thing about yourself, Drew."

The little chuckle that escaped his lips indicated he could see right through her, but she looked at him, coolly expectant. "My bio isn't the most scintillating," he said. "But here's our food. As an accompaniment to the clink of forks and knives, I can give you the bare outlines."

Her steak was so succulently tender, butter-soft in consistency and seasoned to perfection, that she was happy to let Drew supply all conversation for the moment. Her asparagus tips, in a creamy hollandaise, were a work of culinary art, the new potatoes simply prepared but exquisite. There was indeed something to be said for the finer dividends of success, but whatever it was, her mouth was too full to articulate.

"I don't come from a well-to-do family," Drew was saying. "We weren't poor, but it was touch and go for a lot of my growing years. My dad was a partner in a small business that never could seem to stabilize itself—a sporting goods concern in Connecticut, sort of a modest local L. L. Bean?"

Sabrina nodded, content to listen and chew.

"By the time I was old enough to understand what an inept—if well-meaning—businessman my dad was, he was bankrupt. Then came the tough part." He took a sip of wine, nodding at Sabrina's questioning look. "What I mean is, tough for him as well as for us. Businesses in America are always looking for fresh blood—an older man trying to join the work force isn't exactly welcomed with open arms. My mother began to teach at the local high school, and Dad drifted from one job to another, always doing less—and earning less—than he could have." Drew shook his head. "The one thing I knew when I graduated from high school was that I wasn't going to make the same mistake. I had an overwhelming and well-motivated need to figure out why people couldn't handle their own businesses and make them work. So I ended up going for my M.B.A.—at Wharton."

"But you went to Princeton first, didn't you?"

Drew nodded, swallowed a forkful of salmon, then went on. "I was majoring in sociology there, and holding down three jobs to help pay the tuition—"

"Three?"

"All part-time, but I didn't sleep much, it's true. One of them was doing office and clerical work for a psychiatrist, a Dr. Herman, a fascinating man. He taught me a lot about the way people work, on the inside, that is." Drew finished off his glass and began pouring them each another.

"Some of the insights I gained from him steered me away

from getting a graduate degree at Princeton. I opted for business school and learned everything I could about administration and management. I was already writing, theorizing... You see, the thing about business management, so far as I could see, was that it seemed to operate on an almost un-human level. I mean, the so-called human factor was rarely taken into account, really absorbed into the way things were run. You'd see a chain of people unhappy to be working for unhappy people, and nobody really connecting..." He paused, then smiled at Sabrina. "You've heard one of my speeches, so I don't have to bore you with this kind of talk. The gist of it is, I've been trying to forge a link between basic human psychology and better business practices."

"And you've done it, it seems," she said. "Is your dad retired now?"

Drew inspected his wineglass stem. "He died of a heart attack some years back," he said quietly. "But I did get to share at least the beginnings of my smallish fortune with him before he went."

There was silence at their table. "I ought to send a copy of your book to *my* dad," Sabrina said at length. "He doesn't deal with people as people at all, it seems—just as dollar signs."

"What does he do?"

"He's a banker."

"And your mom?"

"She's my mom," she said, putting down her silverware. "And now an accountant. She works in real estate primarily."

"Well, then your folks managed a two-career household."

"Hardly." Sabrina swallowed, then went on. "They've been divorced for thirteen years. My dad couldn't abide my mother doing anything other than pampering him and raising me."

Drew raised an eyebrow. "Do I detect a syndrome of some sort here?"

"I've had a little therapy myself," Sabrina told him. "So spare me any analysis. Yes, Wayne was very much like my father—domineering, opinionated, and obsessed with making big, big bucks. Is it all computing neatly? And, of course, I have an abiding distrust of the male species, and I no longer believe in committed relationships. You see? A textbook case."

"Funny," Drew said, his eyes once again making her feel some indefinable mixture of arousal and apprehension. "When I got burned, I emerged with ideals unscathed."

"What do you mean?"

"I was nearly married once," he said, and she sensed for the first time that the nature of their conversation might be as sensitive to him as it was to her. "I was involved with a woman who was a fast-rising advertising executive. She couldn't handle her career and me at the same time. But when the wounds healed, I was only more determined to find someone who could commit—to having it all."

"I guess you're made of sterner stuff," she said, and, trying to keep the conversation light, made a mock toast. "Here's to your getting it all, and to me getting enough— on my own."

"Why don't we toast to us both getting what we really want?" he suggested, his eyes twinkling. "Keeping it general will make the wine go down smoother, I think."

"Fine," she said, and their glasses clinked.

"But, Sabrina," he went on, after they savored the wine in silence for a moment, "I don't think a person can really go through life solo and find happiness."

"I do," she said, never having felt as uncertain of that sentiment as she did now, looking into Drew's soft, seductive eyes. "Certainly, in today's world, a woman's earning power is increasing," she said, determined to avoid touching on the more personal issues his statement had hinted at. "I don't need a man's support, and I'm happier without it. There's always a trade-off, a compromise."

"Always?"

The husky resonances of his one spoken word seemed to caress her ears. She struggled to remain detached as his eyes gently probed hers. She felt nearly schizophrenic in this conversation—a part of her was all rationality, an automatic pilot, spouting the words she duly lived by, while some irrational, emotional inner being stirred and squirmed beneath Drew's frank appraisal.

"My father thinks that if he sends me money, I'll like him better, love him more. Wayne's angry that I won't take alimony—payments that would make him feel less guilty if I took them, that would imply I needed his help to survive. Well, I don't. I don't need help from anyone."

"No woman's an island," said Drew with a boyish grin.

Sabrina sighed. "You can't stand it, can you? A woman of independent means—you have to disbelieve me to assuage your ego."

"I can stand you fine," he said. "And my ego's in good shape," he added breezily, signaling the waiter. "Interested in dessert?"

She was, even though the meal had been deliciously filling. Drew guided the conversation into shallower waters. She sensed him taking some pressure off. He was shifting gears, it seemed, and was less pointed in his pursuit of her. They began discussing the arts.

He wasn't showy about it, but Drew Dalton had a keenly honed intellect. He was knowledgeable about areas in literature Sabrina never would have suspected him to be. As they crossed swords on favorite authors—he favored the Russians, "big" classics, and Joseph Conrad, whereas she liked the more modern work of Bellow, Doris Lessing, Ann Beattie—she began to fully relax. By now the elegant, romantic atmosphere had worked its soothing charms. Maybe it was hypocritical, but she felt she so rarely got taken out in quite such high style that she figured she might as well enjoy it.

And she was enjoying, in spite of herself, the subtler pleasures of Drew's seductive style. The undercurrent of erotic chemistry between them that she could no longer ignore was simmering right beneath the surface of their conversation, a debate on the merits of a good old-fashioned mystery versus higher forms of literature. She was even allowing herself to let go a little, to revel in the flattery of his appreciative gaze, to flirt back—ever so slightly—in kind. It was all a game, a casual, meaningless amusement, permissible because she knew it would all be over at the evening's end.

"Have you tried Robert Ludlum?" he asked as the waiter brought more coffee to chase down the remains of their delectable chocolate mousses.

She shook her head. "I read one halfway and gave it up. Too..."

"Macho?" he suggested.

Sabrina laughed. "I guess. But it was more the preposterous plot."

"I know," he nodded. "Don't look now, there's a Communist agent in your bathtub—they're all like that. I prefer John Le Carré."

"Umm," she agreed, nodding vehemently. "I wish I'd seen that TV movie they made of his last book, the one with Alec Guinness. I missed it."

"I've got it on tape," Drew said. "Come on over and I'll run it for you. I wouldn't mind watching it again."

She was about to accept this open invitation enthusiastically when she caught herself. What was she thinking of? She hadn't planned on seeing Drew Dalton again, not socially at least. She'd made it clear in their earlier conversation that she didn't want to get involved with him...hadn't she?

But now he was intimating a future for them, and she had to admit there was a good deal to like about Drew. It was a vexing concept, liking Drew. She wondered if they could be...what? Friends? How was one to become "friends" with a man like him? And how did she know this low-key approach wasn't just another subversive method, keeping things "casual" until he insinuated himself right into her bed?

"Well, maybe sometime," was her vague and evasive reply to Drew's offer. She avoided his eyes, turning her attention to the dramatic vista outside the window. Some of the buildings across the river were dark now, some half-lit in random glittering patterns. Long, wispy blue-gray clouds scudded across the starlit sky, some pinpoints of light moving, airplane headlights that the choppy water below scattered in reflection. From here the big city looked small enough to hold in one's hand. She stole a glance at Drew and caught him in profile, looking at the view as well. His serene stare, the strong cheekbones, and the thrust of his chin gave him an air of nobility. He could have been a prince surveying his domain.

Drew must have felt her eyes on him. He turned slightly, and conveyed with a tilt of his head and the hint of a smile his pleasure in the view—and in sharing the moment with her. Sabrina felt a shiver of indescribably sweet excitement stir in her depths, a strange, poignant longing in its wake.

She tore her eyes from Drew's, thankful that their waiter had once again materialized. All of this expensive wine and food was obviously going to her head. When Drew asked if she was interested in cognac, she demurred, suddenly almost desperate to be out of the restaurant and back in the safety of her apartment, alone.

The ride back was largely uneventful. Drew joked and kidded her out of what threatened to be a pensive and non-communicative mood. Sabrina was rattled. She'd come prepared to have an awful time, and the awful thing was, she'd thoroughly enjoyed herself. Now, as they wended their way uptown, she was in a state of emotional confusion. He seemed to know her too well already, and he barely knew her at all . . .

"So what else do you hate about New York—besides the noise, the pollution, the snobbery, the proliferation of men who do eat quiche and take Woody Allen very seriously?"

Sabrina laughed. "New Yorkers know absolutely nothing about Mexican food. And in California—"

"It goes without saying. Are you a cook?"

"I make a decent hamburger," she told him.

"Lots of onions?"

"I am an onion eater," she admitted with mock solemnity.

"I'm an onion *lover*," he said with equal gravity. "I even know a recipe for onion soup."

"You cook?" she said, incredulous. "Don't you have a live-in chef or something?"

Drew shook his head. "No, I have French food flown in every night on the Concorde. Just how wealthy do you think I am?"

"I think you're doing okay."

"Is there something wrong with that?" His tone was one of genuine puzzlement, and she felt sorry that she was continuing to needle him about it.

"No," she said. "Maybe I'm a little jealous, or..."

"...or used to resenting men with sizable incomes," he finished. "Well, at least I can rest assured you're not after me for my money."

"I'm not after you at all," she reminded him.

"I know," he said with a grin. "It makes this all the more interesting."

"This?" she said. "This what?"

"This romance."

His offhand tone reverberated oddly in the quiet, plush interior of the car. Sabrina stared at him.

"This," she said evenly, "is not a romance."

"No?" They were a block or so away from her apartment, and Drew was checking the street numbers. "What would you call it?"

"The fulfillment of a contractual obligation," she said coolly.

"You don't feel anything... out of the ordinary going

on?" He slowed the car to a halt at the curb outside her building, turning to look at her in the dim light.

"The only thing out of the ordinary about this situation is your painfully overwrought imagination," she said.

He smiled. "You feel it," he said. "I know you do."

She bristled with irritation at his smug complacency. "I feel nothing but full," she told him. "The dinner was delicious, by the way, and thank you. Now, if you'll just give me a clue as to how I can extricate myself from this contraption—" Her hand was searching in vain on the inside of the door for some recognizable handle.

"I'll get it," Drew said, and had his own door open in the blink of an eye. She sat in the seat listening to her blood boil as he came around to open her door. Her first impression had been right—the man was simply an insufferable egotist.

She tried to lift herself out of the car without taking his proffered arm, but the angle was too awkward. She fell back in her seat. Sabrina took a deep breath. If he was smiling, she might have to hit him.

"Allow me," Drew said smoothly, his countenance a blank.

Scowling, she took hold of his arm and climbed out of the low-slung vehicle, aware that he was looking at her legs. She headed for home, Drew at her side. She resisted an urge to shake him loose with a well-placed elbow, and concentrated on finding her keys in her handbag.

Locating them, she moved away from Drew and hopped up the few steps to the front door of her apartment building. "Good night," she said, in what she hoped would pass for a polite tone.

"Not even a handshake?" He was looking up at her, the wind riffling through his hair, a combination of boyish charm and sophisticated manhood in a tan trench coat, his eyes gleaming with what seemed to be a teasing challenge.

Sabrina sighed and put out her hand. Drew moved closer and grasped her hand in his. She ignored the tremor she felt at his touch and looked him in the eye with steely resolution. "Thanks again," she said, and prepared to turn away.

But Drew wouldn't let go. And as she watched in growing horror, he mounted the steps and quickly stood right next to her, his other arm gliding around her back before she could move. His face hovered inches above hers. "If you don't have any romantic feelings for me whatsoever," he said softly, "then you certainly couldn't find any harm in a friendly good night kiss. Consider it a sop toward dating etiquette."

"Wait a—" she began, but then his mouth came down over hers.

His lips were warm. That was all she knew at first, the warmth of him and the answering heat that rose up within her like an arching flame. And then the wetness of his tongue parted her lips, searching out the inner recesses of her mouth. Her tongue sought his, tasting the salty sweetness, and the warmth blossomed and grew. Her hands, which had come up to push him from her, settled briefly against his chest, then slid upward to grip the lapels of his suit. Her body, with a will of its own, pressed against him, her breasts straining, the tips swelling as his hands moved down to arch her hips forward to meet his. Their tongues were enmeshed in a delirious dance of yearning hunger, and colors danced before her tightly shut eyes. She was breathless, lost in a surge of desire. The raw intensity of it, the heady assault of his tongue and lips, was overpowering.

His lips left hers. Her eyes blinked open.

"Deny it again," he whispered huskily.

She could only stare, waiting for the rest of the world to come into focus beyond his luminous eyes.

"Deny that you feel . . . what I'm feeling for you," he said.

Reality was filtering back into her consciousness. Sabrina swallowed. She let go of the lapels she'd so tightly grasped, and pushed, forcefully, until he released her from his embrace.

She prayed her voice wouldn't shake, that her cheeks weren't already crimson with arousal. "It's that expensive wine," she told him. "It really brings out the tease in me."

Drew's eyes narrowed. "Meaning?"

She tossed her hair back from her face. "Was I convincing? I'm sorry, Drew, but I couldn't help rising to your bait. There, I've fulfilled your little fantasy—a truly romantic good night kiss. Did I give a good performance? I tried awfully hard."

"Did you?" he muttered wryly, studying her face.

"But I think sticking to business from now on is a better idea," she continued blithely. "I'm afraid you'll think of me as too unprofessional otherwise."

"Yeah," he said briskly, and she thought she detected a note of resignation in his voice. "We can't have that."

"No," she said, and gave him a bright smile. "Well, good night." She turned, fitting the key into the lock of the lobby door.

"Sabrina."

She turned. Drew was smiling again. "Yes?"

"You really are extraordinary," he said. "That *was* a great performance—academy all the way. Especially," he added meaningfully with an insolent grin, "your dialogue. That little speech afterward was priceless." He gave her a jaunty wave and headed for his car.

Grinding her teeth, Sabrina entered her building and took the elevator upstairs. But once she was inside her apartment her anger faded, and she was suddenly unaccountably forlorn. Deflated, she sank listlessly onto her bed. Van Dyke climbed up to say hello. "I'm not lonely," she informed the cat. "I'm just alone by choice," she added. But even he appeared to disbelieve her.

5

"WELL?"

Sabrina looked up from her desk. Lydia was hovering, her coat still on but a cigarette already lit. A newspaper was tucked under her arm and she had a very expectant look on her face.

"I've just started taking messages off the service," Sabrina told her. "Cathy's not in yet. Nothing important so far—"

"No, no, no," Lydia said impatiently. "How was it?"

"How was what?"

Lydia exhaled a puff of smoke exasperatedly. "Your date! With Drew Dalton—it *was* Friday night, wasn't it?"

"Well, yes," Sabrina said, a little startled by the intensity of Lydia's interest. "It was."

"Was what?"

Sabrina considered her reply carefully. "It was an experience..." she began.

"I'll bet," said Lydia.

"...not altogether unpleasant..."

"His place or yours?"

"Neither!" Sabrina's eyes widened.

"Really?" Lydia settled into the chair by Sabrina's desk with an expression of renewed curiosity. "Where then?"

"Lydia," Sabrina explained, shocked. "Nothing happened—like that."

"Oh," Lydia said, seemingly crestfallen. "And here I thought you might have spent the weekend—you know." She nodded her head in the direction of the window. "I had many pleasant images of you ensconced in that penthouse while I played bridge with my in-laws."

"I don't believe this," Sabrina muttered. "You're disappointed?"

"Well, your mother will be," Lydia murmured, then caught herself too late. "I mean—"

"My mother?" Sabrina's voice rose. "What does she have to—" She stopped, seeing the telltale guilty look on Lydia's face. "Oh," she said dryly. "The wires have been humming."

"Well, I did happen to mention that you were going out with one of the most attractive eligible bachelors in the city of New York when she—" Lydia stopped, wavering beneath Sabrina's stern gaze. "—when I called her last week," she finished. "So, naturally..."

"So naturally the two of you have gotten me engaged, married, and—am I expecting yet? Grandchildren on the way?"

"Now, Sabrina. I don't think it's unnatural for your mother to be a little concerned. It's been almost two years since your divorce."

"Barely a year and a half," Sabrina said grimly. "That's hardly any time at all."

"Youth is truly wasted on the young." Lydia sighed.

"What I could have done with a year and a half of singledom at your age!" She got up from the chair, gingerly holding her long-ashed butt. Sabrina pushed an ashtray toward her. "He didn't make a pass at you?"

Sabrina clapped a hand to her face. "You want a blow-by-blow? I think if he ever asks me out again, I'll send you along as a substitute. I have a feeling you'd enjoy it more than I did."

Lydia shrugged. "He's not your type?"

"No. Well, maybe too much so. I mean..." Her voice trailed off, and she looked away, embarrassed.

"Ah," said Lydia. There was a pregnant silence as she stubbed out her cigarette. Lydia walked to the door, then turned back before leaving the little room, her eyes twinkling. "Just don't play *too* hard to get."

Before she could think of a suitable reply, Lydia was gone. Sabrina sat back in her chair, glaring at the ashtray. She heard the outer office door open and Cathy's cheery voice. She listened to the sounds of activity all around her, but remained momentarily immobile, her eyes slowly drawn to the closed blinds on her window. When she realized that she was burning a hole through the blinds with her steady stare, she jolted back into action, sitting up straight and turning her attention to organizing her cluttered desk.

There was no use pretending that her date with Drew Dalton had had no effect on her. Much of Sabrina's weekend had been spent in a listless, lethargic fashion, as if her experience Friday night had sapped all of her energy.

She checked her notes, mentally assigning priorities for phone calls and letters that had to be taken care of. But a part of her was still at the Riverview feeling Drew's eyes bathe her in a warm, special glow. She organized a file, left messages for two prominent meeting planners, and spoke briefly with a prospective client. But a part of her was still standing on the steps of her building, wrapped in Drew's arms.

Stop it, she commanded herself. It was bad enough that

the man had been in her thoughts throughout the weekend, but she had work to do. She sighed. In the time alone at home she'd actually wondered if she'd made a mistake. Maybe she shouldn't have pushed him away from her, and tried to mock her own emotions and his. Why was she so hell-bent on depriving herself of his companionship, when . . .

She needed it? Sabrina stared at the blinds again. Ridiculous. Now, in the cool, clear light of day, such an idea seemed preposterous. Sooner or later she'd find the male companionship she sought—on her own terms, and in her own good time. Drew Dalton was exactly what she didn't need. If there had been any attraction, it had been purely sexual—and didn't she know better than to confuse that with her deeper feelings? It could be the situation with Wayne all over again . . . No, she'd done the right thing. Hopefully that was the end of it, and she could get back on track.

"Package for you, Sabrina—and these."

Cathy was in the doorway, a small bouquet of roses wrapped in colored paper in one hand and a gift-wrapped parcel in the other. With a sinking sensation Sabrina accepted both, ignoring Cathy's teasing comments about secret admirers. She unwrapped the gift. It was a book—*The Actor's Primer*—written by a well-known East Coast thespian. The inscription, written on the flyleaf in a bold but neat, unmistakably masculine hand, read: "Keep up the good work! And here's to a return performance—D.D."

Her intercom buzzed. "Pick up on oh-one, dear," rasped Lydia.

"Sabrina Hamilton," she said tersely.

"Good morning," said Drew. "Have a nice weekend?"

"Fine, thank you," she said through clenched teeth.

"Tough morning?" His tone was maddeningly congenial.

"Not at all. I've just spent a leisurely half hour putting unsolicited deliveries through the paper shredder. I'm ankle-deep in rose petals and binding bits."

"Ouch," said Drew. "Where's your sense of humor?"

"Someplace far removed from yours," she said. "Look, I have a lot of work to do—"

"Me, too," he chimed in. "So I'm trying to set aside some leisure time well in advance. How's your Saturday night looking?"

"It's looking filled-in."

"Sunday brunch?"

"Ditto."

"Say, you're not seeing someone else, are you?"

"Someone else? I'm not seeing anyone," she retorted, realizing what she'd said a moment too late. "That is, I'm not seeing you."

"Then who's filling up your Saturday and Sunday?" he persisted, unfazed.

"It's none of your business," she said sharply. "Drew, didn't I make it clear the other night that I had no intention of going out with you again?"

"Not exactly," he said. "Things got a little fuzzy in the home stretch."

"Have your eyes checked," she suggested. "Or your ears cleaned. It was a delightful dinner—though I resent having been coerced into it—and now that everything's settled, let's stick to business."

"All right," he said breezily. "I need an information update sheet on the booking for the twenty-seventh. Normally you could send it to Sandy, but since I'm right across the street, you can messenger it direct. Can I get it by the end of the day?"

"What booking on the twenty-seventh?" she said, startled.

He clucked his tongue. "One of the first principles of management in a small office such as yours is the proper distribution of duties—along with a quick dissemination of information. In other words, how come one hand doesn't know what the other is doing? Didn't Lydia tell you?"

"Excuse me," she said, reddening. "There's a call on the other line. I'll have to get back to you."

"Fine," he said. "I'll be right here."

"How comforting," she snarled after slamming down the receiver. "Lydia!" She rose quickly from her desk and headed for the other office.

"Look," Lydia said, blowing a smoke ring as Sabrina paced angrily around the room. "Word is out. We've got a men's division. Who am I to turn down a reasonable—and lucrative—offer?"

"Annette Powers would be perfect for a collegiate seminar on management strategy," Sabrina stormed. "Why Drew?"

"Well, truthfully, Sabrina, his was the first name that came to mind."

"I can't imagine why!"

Lydia gave Sabrina a withering look over the top of her reading glasses. "And what is that supposed to mean, dear?"

"It just strikes me as coincidental," she answered grimly.

"Well, Drew Dalton happens to be a Princeton alumnus," Lydia said. "Mr. Halyrod, the college meeting planner, took to the idea immediately."

"Sarah Hughes is a Vassar graduate," Sabrina said. "Why not—"

"Sabrina, they were more interested in a man. And they were more than interested in Drew. In fact, they salivated. We're going to have to face the facts—Drew is a draw."

Sabrina stood by Lydia's desk, her arms folded. The two women looked at each other in silence. "Tell me one thing," Sabrina said quietly. "Why didn't you consult me first? I had no idea you'd gone ahead and called Dalton this morning. The next thing I know, he's on the line with me, talking about a booking I had no idea existed."

Lydia took a final puff of her cigarette and stubbed it out. "To tell you the truth, dear, I was afraid you'd give me a hard time—like this. And I was more interested in nailing the booking quickly. Now I've sold Drew, the booking's solid, and I don't see why it makes a difference. It shouldn't," she added firmly as Sabrina opened her mouth to protest. "Besides, with the bills we have outstanding from moving into this office, any dates we can pull in are a blessing. Why, the costs of those blinds alone—"

"All right, all right," Sabrina said crossly. Lydia knew that the one way to get Sabrina off her back was to recite a litany of their sad financial state. Sabrina immediately recognized the ploy, but wasn't in the mood for arguing anymore.

"One thing, dear," Lydia said as Sabrina headed for the door.

"Yes?"

"Dalton's an automatic moneymaker. Every appearance he makes is an instant advertisement for Evans. We've already gotten some calls from other male speakers who've expressed interest in using us. So, please, Sabrina"—she looked at the young woman imploringly—"let's try to take the most positive tack with this. Personal feelings aside," she said pointedly.

"You're the boss," Sabrina said.

Arrangements were made. There were calls from Sandy O'Byrne every few days to go over one detail or another, but Sabrina didn't speak to Drew directly. Inexplicably he seemed to have receded into the background, withdrawing from his persistent pursuit of her. She found herself asking the agent, after a week or so had gone by, if Drew was out of town. Sandy said that he was, but that he was expected back shortly. Was there something Sandy could help her with?

No. No one could help her with the particular problem that began to plague her. It snuck in between the cracks of increasingly busy days stuffed full of phone calls, appointments, designing and putting together a new mailing that boasted of Evans's new division, now a paltry but respectable eight men strong. It clouded the periphery of her consciousness when she was alone, and insinuated itself into her thoughts when she was out with friends. The problem was Drew, or, rather, ironically enough, his disappearance.

Far from being relieved that his persistent annoying phone calls had abruptly halted, Sabrina was now irked by his silence. Somehow she'd assumed he would dog her stubbornly, not take no for an answer. She should have been glad his attentions had ceased. Instead, she was irrationally irritated. It wasn't as if his presence weren't felt and could be easily shunted off either. Every day she came to work her eyes would steal to the building top across the way. When she exited and entered her own building her gaze would be automatically drawn to that gleaming penthouse. She'd taken to leaving her blinds up, once informed that Drew was out of town—and she kept them up, consciously a defiance, and unconsciously... an invitation?

Her mother even inquired about him in a Sunday phone call, Lydia having duly informed her of the progress—or lack thereof—in her junior partner's "new relationship."

"It's not a relationship," she told her mother, exasperated. "We went out once. I wasn't interested."

"A handsome fellow," her mother observed. "And he writes well."

"You read that—that overblown pamphlet of his?"

"Well, everyone has, dear. Haven't you?"

"I haven't had a minute to spare," she said caustically.

"I suppose not," her mother went on. "If you don't even have time to go out with an attractive young man—"

"Mother," she said. "I nipped it in the bud, whatever *it* was. Don't worry about me. If I do get involved with someone, you'll be the first to know—or, knowing Lydia, you'll probably know about it before I do."

By the time Drew's Princeton engagement was a week away, Sabrina had put the whole experience behind her. After all, what had it been? A few encounters, a dance, a few kisses... That had threatened her stability, true, but the crisis had passed and could now be made the stuff of amusing anecdotes. But her stability became more than threatened the Monday before Drew's booking.

"He has to *what?*" she nearly yelled into the phone, her whitened knuckles gripping the receiver tighter.

"He has to cancel," Sandy O'Byrne repeated. "At least it looks that way. You see, the senator needs him to attend that Washington conference all day Friday—and knowing the way senate committees work, I wouldn't count on him being free until six o'clock or so."

It had never occurred to her, prior to this disastrous turn of events, that economists in Washington would consider Drew Dalton such an expert on management stategies that his presence would be summarily required at a Capitol Hill powwow. But D.C. was calling, and Sandy O'Byrne wasn't about to let Drew refuse the call, contract or no contract.

"We can book him a flight out of Washington," she said, thinking out loud. "Hopefully direct to Newark airport—"

"Well," Sandy interrupted. "You're still cutting it too close. The speech is scheduled for eight o'clock, yes?"

"We'll have them move it back an hour." She was in a panic, but it was the kind of panic she could deal with, consisting as it did of a steady stream of adrenaline inducing an almost serene state of hyperawareness in her. Her mind began zipping along in a computerlike fashion.

"Even so, how does he get from Newark to Princeton? That's another hour by car."

"There must be a shuttle to a smaller airport nearby."

"Could be," O'Byrne muttered, sounding dubious.

"Sandy, Drew Dalton is going to speak at Princeton Friday night. I don't care if we have to—" She stopped, struck with a thought.

"Have to what?"

"Helicopter him in," she said. "Hold everything. I'll get back to you within the hour."

A dozen phone calls later, things were falling into place.

With Lydia's help they booked the flight from Washington to Newark, and the helicopter from Newark to Princeton, at a whopping twelve hundred dollars total, thus effectively wiping out any profit they might have realized from the engagement. There was only one small problem.

"Where do you want it to land?" the helicopter rental office wanted to know. "The nearest airfield to the university's still twenty minutes from campus."

"That's twenty minutes we can't lose," Sabrina told Lydia as she paced the office. "The Princeton people are already apoplectic about moving the speech to nine. If we can't guarantee them Drew at a quarter to, *they'll* cancel."

"Stuey Sherman," Lydia said, stubbing out a cigarette with sudden excitement.

"Who?"

"Stu Sherman is the head track and field coordinator up there, and he's an old friend of my husband's. We'll get permission to land on a soccer field or something."

Old friends or no, Stuey Sherman wasn't crazy about a helicopter landing on one of his lovingly tended fields. He'd consider it if the president gave his approval.

The secretary to the college's president was amused. She assured Sabrina he would certainly consider their proposal, and put her on hold for an interminable ten minutes. The secretary returned with a negative answer. Sabrina cajoled. Then Lydia wheedled. They at last got through to the man himself.

The president, as her father used to say, took the long way round the barn. He liked to talk. It took every ounce of Sabrina's calculated charm to keep him on the subject proper and butter him up properly at the same time. He allowed that the speech was an important function. And yes, Drew was a prestigious alumnus. In fact, he remembered that when Drew had attended Princeton he'd shown signs of unusual promise...

After wading through twenty minutes of academic rhetoric, Sabrina at last got an affirmative answer. The helicopter could land on the older of the two football fields, not a two-minute walk from the hall where Drew was scheduled to speak.

Sandy O'Byrne received the news of their hard and frenzied labor with characteristic ebullience. "Nice," he said. "That should work."

"You're sure he can make the six-forty flight?"

"I can't see the meeting going past six," Sandy said. "And even so, Drew would rather honor his commitment than not. He'll make the flight. There's one other thing though—how's he getting from Princeton back to New York?"

"Well, we had a limo booked for him," Sabrina said, watching Lydia shake her head sadly as she spoke. "We'll just rebook a one-way from the New Jersey end, I guess."

When she hung up Lydia was gazing balefully at her pocket calculator. "We're already in the red over this sorry mess," she said. "That limo's going to be another two hundred." She sighed. "We simply can't afford to spend another penny."

"I knew Drew Dalton was going to be one giant headache ever since I got involved with him," Sabrina said.

"We," said Lydia. "*We* got involved."

"Hmm?"

"You said *I*," Lydia noted with a sage smile. "Your Freudian slip is showing."

"Look," said Sabrina. "This is business. I don't care about Drew Dalton personally one way or another."

"No?" Lydia lit another cigarette, then peered over her eyeglasses at Sabrina. "That's good. Because you're going to drive my car up to Princeton and chauffeur that guy back here for no more than the cost of a tank of gas. If he can consider backing out on us because some cabinet member needs his hand held, then he can do without a limousine."

"Me?" Sabrina stared at her, outraged. "Why me?"

"I've got a dinner with the WJA people Friday night," Lydia said. "And besides, I can't drive at night." She tapped her glasses with her forefinger. "Last time I took the wheel after sundown I nearly totalled Henry's Volkswagen."

"But—but—"

"You love to drive," Lydia went on, oblivious to Sabrina's sputters of protest. "You're always complaining that you miss the open roads of sunny California. Now you can experience the wonders of the New Jersey Turnpike. And truthfully, what with helicopters and all that flying around up there, I'd feel a lot safer about this booking if you were there to oversee it."

"You would, would you?" Sabrina said. "If I didn't know better, I'd think you engineered this imbroglio yourself."

"Strange are the ways..." Lydia smiled.

"Spare me," Sabrina pleaded.

"I can hear it!" called a voice.

"I see it!" yelled another.

Sabrina craned her neck, searching the sky as the wind whipped her hair about her face. Now she, too, could hear the metallic buzz and whir of the approaching helicopter's blades. A hearty group of Princeton men were gathered on the field around her, some arrayed at either end waving flashlights. Earlier, a few eager sophomores had strung large high-beam lights atop the goalposts to form a makeshift landing beacon.

Now, a studious-looking but authoritative senior who had been helping Sabrina organize things since her arrival an hour before hustled her unceremoniously back from the goal line. The helicopter was hovering, it own headlights blinding, the flurry of wind even stronger now. Slowly it descended in a diagonal line and then, amid spontaneous cheers and applause from all the students, touched ground.

Mr. Halyrod, the Princeton meeting planner, hurried forward, his bald pate gleaming in the harsh beams. The helicopter's door swung open from within, and Drew Dalton emerged, his tall, rangy form bent over beneath the whirring copter blades.

It would have been a dramatic entrance for any man, but the sight of Drew, his hair disheveled in the wind, his lean body in the sharp-lined trench coat silhouetted in the helicopter's lights, caused a tremor of excitement to course through Sabrina. She told herself it was the piercing wind that made her shiver as she watched him approach. Mr. Halyrod was gesturing and talking, dwarfed at the taller man's side, but Drew was scanning the faces around him. Some students in front of her moved suddenly, and his eyes found hers. His chiseled features relaxed into a warm smile, his eyes twinkling as he came closer and her heartbeat picked up speed.

"Hi, there," he said as casually as if they'd seen each other the day before. Actually over a month had passed since their date. Sabrina flinched as he easily and naturally took hold of her arm, propelling her forward alongside Mr. Halyrod. Her mind, which on the long drive to Princeton had been teeming with witty remarks, was suddenly blank. Her concentration was skewed by the electric surge of energy she felt as she walked close by Drew's side. The strong wind seemed to lighten her step, as though she were borne aloft by the air.

"How was Washington?" she asked, trying to match his casual tone. Was he going to pretend, now, that nothing had gone on between them?

"They don't know *what* they're doing down there," he said ruefully.

"But you set them straight, I suppose."

Drew grinned. "I did my best."

"It's this way," Mr. Halyrod said, steering them down a winding slatestone path toward an ivy-covered building that loomed ahead. A small group of students was following right behind them, and Sabrina could see more of them as well as faculty members waiting to greet them on the steps of the hall. Flurries of fallen leaves whistled and crunched in their wake and scattered in their path. Drew's arm was draped lightly around her shoulders as they walked down a slight incline. Sabrina both resented and welcomed this gesture of familiarity. She had an impulse to move away from him, but the stronger impulse was to stay.

"You must be happy to see me," he said.

Sabrina stared up at his face. She knew him well enough by now to recognize the impish sparkle in his eye that signaled provocation even as the rest of his face betrayed nothing but innocent intentions.

"Yes, I was worried that you'd miss the plane," she said, keeping her own features blandly indifferent.

"Are you ready for me?" he went on, the sparkle in his eyes joined now by the hint of a devilish smile at the corners of his mouth.

"It's a packed house," she said dryly. "Everything's been set up. We've even got ten minutes for you to prepare yourself."

"I'm prepared," he said, and there was no mistaking a deliberate second meaning behind his words as Drew's eyes caressed hers briefly but meaningfully, then roved quickly over her figure.

"Here we are then," Mr. Halyrod was saying.

Drew was greeted by a professor who had obviously tutored him years before. Sabrina stayed close by, seeing to it that no one delayed the speaker unnecessarily as they made their way to the little dressing room off the main auditorium. She'd made sure that a pitcher of ice water and a glass were there for him, and located the nearest washroom, which she pointed out to Drew as they paused at the dressing room door.

"I'll knock in another five minutes," she told him.

"Fine," he said, but he caught her wrist as she turned to go, and gently but firmly pulled her closer. "Sabrina," he murmured.

"What?" She gazed up into his eyes, feeling the soft pull of their velvet depths. She had the strange sensation he was looking for something within her, and then some undefinable emotion rose inside of her, unbidden, in response to his unvoiced question.

His eyes widened almost imperceptibly, their glow a little brighter. "What?" she repeated dumbly, her voice huskier than she'd intended.

"Just looking," he said slowly, then released her wrist.

Sabrina swallowed, shrugged, and turned, her wrist tingling, a sudden flurry of butterflies loose in her stomach. "Be right back," she called over her shoulder. She heard the door shut as she walked quickly down the hall, feeling a flush in her cheeks. Forget the witty and scathing remarks; being with Drew was tying her tongue in knots. Sabrina smoothed her hair back from her face as she approached the side door of the auditorium. She was overwound from the drive and the tense preparations, that was all. Now that the unknown factors were taken care of and everything was going smoothly, she could relax. There was just the speech. A glance around the auditorium informed her that every seat was taken, and knowing Drew, the speech would be splendid—the least of her worries. Then there would be some question and answers, autographing, perhaps a quick bite, and the drive home.

With that last little detail to think about, relaxation was a lost cause.

Princeton welcomed its alumnus with hearty applause, and an hour and fifteen minutes later the applause was thunderous. Drew lingered more than Sabrina had expected him to, greeting old acquaintances and chatting with students. He seemed to be thoroughly enjoying himself, and it looked to her that rather than being exhausted by his long day and night's activities, he was thriving on them.

A small buffet had been set up in the reception area downstairs. Drew and some faculty members munched on cold cuts and Sabrina did the same, allowing herself a glass of white wine to calm her nerves. Then Drew took his leave. Sabrina gave him a few minutes to change, then knocked on the door to his little room.

"Come in."

Sabrina walked in, then froze, the door swinging shut softly behind her. Drew was naked to the waist, his back to her as he removed a clean shirt from his hanging carry-all. She stared at the smooth bronze skin, sculpted muscles rippling in his forearms, and shoulders of finely corded sinew. Then he turned, and she was unable to lift her eyes fast enough from the delicate whorls of fine dark hair that covered his chest, his trim, flat stomach, descending in little spirals into his trousers.

"So what do you think?" he said, shirt in hand.

Sabrina tried to stem the flow of blood into her cheeks. "You're in pretty good shape, she said. "Does your pent-house have a gym?"

Drew laughed, slipping into his soft blue button-down. "No, I mean what do you think—did it go okay? Everyone happy?"

"It was very successful," she said, flushing violently. How could she have mistaken the intent of his words? It certainly showed him where her thoughts lay! Quickly she turned to the door. "I'll just wait outside."

Drew joined her in the hall a few minutes later, straightening his blazer and ready to go, suitbag in hand. "Success looks good on you," he murmured in her ear. "Puts color in your cheeks."

Before she could respond, Mr. Halyrod had joined them. The administrator then accompanied them to the parking lot. Sabrina made sure to thank him profusely for his help. Drew said his good-byes to the last lingering Princetonians. And then it was just the two of them facing Lydia's car— a Volkswagen that had seen better days but had nonetheless gotten Sabrina to the campus in good time. Its gearshift was worn, with a tendency to slip out of second, but Sabrina, used to the challenges of the San Francisco hills, found handling the car on the relatively flat roads of Jersey no problem.

"Your limo, Mr. Dalton," she said.

"Cutting a few corners, eh?" He opened the door, shoving his bag into the back.

"Your patriotic sojourn had some serious financial repercussions," she said, getting into the car.

"Sorry about that," he said, closing his door after him. She gunned the motor, turned on the lights, and gave the engine a chance to warm up, conscious that Drew was watching her.

"Don't worry, you're in capable hands," she told him.

"Being in your hands sounds good to me," he said.

Sabrina cleared her throat and put the car into gear. Soon they were out of the lot and on the road. "There's a little map in the glove compartment," she said. "Can you tell me where the turnoff for the turnpike is? I think we go three lights down this road and take a left at the fork."

"That's right," Drew said after squinting at the piece of paper. They both sat in silence for a stretch. The whistle of the wind was consistent, as was the motor's steady rumble. There weren't many other cars on the road at this time of night. She glanced at her watch. Eleven-forty. Even with good time the city was two hours away.

"This your car?"

"Lydia's," she answered. "I realize it's not the latest in technology, but it'll get us there."

He nodded. "How's Evans Speaker Resources?"

"Just fine," she said warily, not wanting to discuss the intricacies of their business with this ever-critical expert.

"Evans Speaker Resources," he repeated. "Speaker Resources..." he muttered to himself. "Too many syllables," he pronounced suddenly. "Have you ever considered shortening the name?"

"No," Sabrina said.

"How about just plain Evans Speakers? The Resources is really superfluous."

Sabrina's hands tightened on the steering wheel. It was going to be a long drive. "How about leaving our name alone?" she asked with ice-edged sweetness. "Your input is really unnecessary."

"Just thinking out loud," he said. "Shorter names usually increase a company's recognition factor—"

"Spare me," she interrupted. "We're happy with our name."

"Well, maybe after you've been in business awhile—"

"We like our name," she began, trying to keep her voice level. "It pleases us. We have letterheads nicely designed to accommodate it. No one has ever forgotten it. It rolls trippingly off the tongue. It looks nice on our doorplate. We are not about to change it"—her voice was rising. With effort, she curbed her momentum—"so please don't worry yourself about it," she finished, deliberately polite.

"Well," said Drew after a pause, "how are things anyway? At Evans Speaker Resources?"

"Word seems to be out that we're handling men now," Sabrina told him. "We've pulled in a few new clients."

"Did David Hellstrom call you?"

"Yes, and we're going to try to get him some dates."

"And Michael Feibush?"

"Him, too."

"And Matthew Boxt?"

Sabrina shot him a look. "Have you been tapping our phone lines? Or . . ." She stopped, the realization hitting her with a jolt. "How many?" she asked, an edge in her voice.

"Just those. Oh, and Andrew Morrel. You don't mind, do you?"

Sabrina sighed. She might have known that so many prominent men in business wouldn't have called Evans without a little nudge from a prominent acquaintance . . . "I'm not in a position to mind," she said grimly. "But it was

nicer to think that they were calling us of their own volition."
She took a winding curve much too sharply and felt a won-
derfully vindictive satisfaction as Drew lurched forward,
nearly hitting his head against the windshield.

"Sorry," she said.

"Uh-huh," he replied. "We're not in *that* much of a hurry,
are we?"

"I don't want you to lose any beauty sleep," she said
sweetly. "And I'm a little fatigued myself."

"Somehow I felt safer in that helicopter," he muttered.
"Look, Sabrina, I was only being helpful. I figured you
could use some more names to get your division off the
ground, so I talked you up a bit to some friends. What's
wrong with that?"

"Nothing," she said crossly. "But I didn't ask you for
help. And though I'm sure you couldn't conceive of looking
at it that way, the men's division isn't top priority for us.
We're still primarily a women's bureau—a flourishing one,
by the by, before you rode in on your high white horse."
The tires squealed again as she barreled up the ramp to the
turnpike, and Drew fidgeted in his seat, a hand against the
dashboard.

"Speaking of high horses," he said. "Would you like to
tell me how any speaker's bureau survives without indulging
in some old-fashioned word-of-mouth advertisement? Men—
women—what's the difference? What you want to do is
increase your visibility, period."

"Thanks for telling me what I want to do."

"Sabrina—"

"I suppose since you make your living telling people
what they should or shouldn't do, you can't help butting
in. But I'm not one of the millions of dimwits in this country
who are so inept at running their own businesses, they have
to rely on the pabulum you publish to teach them some
common sense."

"Pabulum?" His tone was ominously mild.

"Well, really, Drew—" The words were tumbling out

of her, fueled by her angry indignation at his unsolicited behind-the-scenes manipulations, even though she knew she was rashly crossing the line between professional tact and personal prejudice. "The fact that that book of yours is a number-one best seller is a sad commentary on the intellectual level of the American public."

"It wasn't written for academics or for the literati," he said, the annoyance in his tone increasing.

"Clearly," she snapped.

"Some people aren't as close-minded to hearing some simple truths spelled out in easy language as you seem to be," he said.

"Well, they say there's a sucker born every minute," she said. "That could account for your sales."

"A lot of those so-called suckers are running major corporations," he began. "Who do you think—"

"Look, I just don't need the benefit of your wisdom, okay?" she said hotly. "I'm thoroughly in control of—"

Suddenly the car shook with an abrupt explosion, bolting forward and careening crazily. Startled, Sabrina momentarily lost her grip on the wheel. Drew lunged for it. The car skidded with a sickening screech and a little scream of fear escaped her lips. Then just as suddenly they were jolting and shuddering to a halt in a hail of gravel on the side of the road.

6

SABRINA'S HEART POUNDED in her ears, her body trembling from head to foot. Shocked and bewildered, she didn't hear Drew until the second time he said her name.

"Sabrina, are you all right?"

She nodded, mute, feeling his hand gripping her shoulder. She realized that even while gaining control of the car he'd been holding her back against her seat with his arm.

"I think that's what's properly called a blowout," he said, and slowly released his grip on both her and the wheel. Sabrina took a deep breath and let it out slowly. "Let's take a look," Drew muttered, and opened his door. She followed.

The left rear tire was a misshapen oblong of deflated rubber.

"Hope the rim's okay," said Drew. "Well, let's get the trunk open."

Sabrina reached under the dashboard for the switch, and the front hood popped up an inch. Drew pulled it up and peered in. Thankfully there was a spare tire. Sabrina reached around the edge of it, searching for the jack.

"I'll get that," said Drew.

"I've got it," she said, and pulled the slightly greasy metal contraption free. Drew put his hand out, ready to take it from her, but Sabrina paused. Now that the initial aftershock had worn off, her resentment of him had returned. She was damned if she was going to play the helpless female to his macho Mr. Fix-it.

"You're the passenger and I'm the chauffeur," she reminded him.

"So?"

"So, I'm perfectly capable of changing a tire, though you may find it hard to believe."

Drew stared at her, the edges of his mouth crinkling with amusement. "I'm sure you are," he said. "But I could probably get it done a great deal faster."

"Ha!" she said defiantly. "Just watch me."

She turned abruptly and marched to the rear of the car, jack in hand. In her mind she was hurriedly reviewing the process she'd undertaken only once before, over a half dozen years ago in Los Angeles. She knelt by the back of the car, mentally sighting the right place to put the lip of the metal jack. The gentle crunch of Drew's shoes alerted her to his presence directly behind her.

Sabrina put the jack in place and stood up. It was the kind of jack that had its own lever attached, and she knew that all she'd have to do was pump . . . She looked down at her legs. The stockings would have to go. But Drew was standing close by, an expression of amused interest on his face, his arms folded. Well, cross off a pair of stockings. She'd rather have runs than Drew's salacious scrutiny. She began to crank the lever up and down, gingerly balancing herself with one hand against the car.

It was easy going at first. But as the lip caught the edge

of the car she had to exert some muscle power on the handle. She was determined, though, and with some minimal huffing and puffing was one more stroke away from having the flat high enough off the ground. Suddenly the car wobbled precariously and dropped, the jack falling with a clatter. She caught her balance just in time, averting a pratfall as the only car that had passed them since the blowout slowed to observe her, then moved on.

Something that sounded like a polite cough came from Drew. Sabrina set her lips tightly and picked up the jack. So she'd been a little off when she placed it. Big deal. Silently she put the jack in its upright position, pumped it quickly to within an inch of the fender, then got down on her knees and scrutinized the position carefully before starting to pump again.

This time the jack held. She stood up, breathing heavily, wiping her hands with some satisfaction. Now what? She had to get the hubcap off. She glanced at Drew, who seemed to be enjoying himself hugely. Some passing headlights swept across him, highlighting the little gleam she saw dancing in his eyes.

"You're in pretty good shape yourself," he observed. "Do you have a gym in your office?"

"Stow it," she muttered, and quickly moved around to the front of the car to peer under the hood for the . . . the . . . thing, the metal whatchamacallit you had to use to pry off the hubcap and then unscrew the little screws on the rim. She rummaged around in the semi-darkness until her hands felt the cold iron. Tire iron. That was it. And here it was, a long heavy iron rod with a flat screwdriver tip at one end and a curved bit that acted as a wrench on the other.

Brandishing it triumphantly, she marched back to the hoisted end of the car and with some effort managed to pry the hubcap off the rim. It clattered to the ground and rolled into Drew's calf before he could move out of the way.

"Sorry!" she said, unable to suppress a smile as he hopped backward, holding his leg and muttering oaths.

"Sure you are." He grimaced. "They may shoot horses, but I'll live," he added, backing away as she came toward him with the tire iron in hand.

Sabrina stopped where she was and laughed. "Really, I'm sorry," she said. "I wasn't coming in for the kill. I was just retrieving this." She picked up the hubcap from behind him and returned to the tire, her spirits lifting.

With the wind blowing in an icy shaft through the material of her plaid skirt beneath her overcoat, and Drew's wary eye upon her, his tapping foot indicating a growing impatience, Sabrina hurried to remove the lugs holding the tire in place. By the time she'd dropped the fifth screw inside the inverted hubcap on the ground beside her, her fingers were cold and stiff, and her hand was reddened with the exertion of rotating the tire iron. But she was happy with her progress.

Then, taking a deep breath, she grasped the cold and grimy sides of the tire, struggling to mask her distaste. She sensed Drew hovering at her side, but before he could put a helping hand on the tire she deliberately moved in his way, yanking and pulling.

"Really, Sabrina," he said. "It might go easier with some extra muscle power."

"That's okay," she said tersely, straining to pull the tire loose from the rim. "I've got all the muscle power I—oof!"

The tire was free and she lurched backward. Drew was right behind her, and only his quickly offered support kept her from falling. Her shoulder rammed into his stomach, and this time Drew's sharp intake of breath caused her more embarrassment than satisfaction.

"Thanks," she muttered as he helped her to her feet. Quickly Sabrina walked around to the car's other end and reached into the trunk to pull the spare out. It was too heavy for her to lift easily. Pausing, she glanced at Drew, who was observing her, implacable, holding his trench coat closed tight against the rising wind. With a surge of determined effort she managed to lift the tire high enough to slide it over the edge of the trunk and guide it awkwardly to the ground.

Sabrina took a moment to catch her breath, then wheeled the spare around to the back. Although none of the many cars that had slowed to watch her thus far had stopped to offer any help, one, a dilapidated Plymouth, was lingering now by the side of the road. The driver reached across his seat to roll down the window.

"Need any assistance, lady?" It was a bearded young man in a sweat shirt. He squinted at her, then turned a quizzical eye on Drew.

"No, thanks, I've got it under control," she assured him, leaning the tire against the back fender. The driver was now openly staring at Drew, who gazed back blandly, his arms folded.

"You sure?"

"She's a whiz at this," Drew informed the young man, who narrowed his eyes at Drew, shook his head, and then drove on.

Sabrina, momentarily intent on watching the Plymouth, wasn't fast enough to stop Drew from stepping behind her back and hoisting the tire up onto the rim in one deft motion.

"Hey!" she called out.

"Sorry," he said, fitting the tire snugly in place and then backing away fast, slapping the dirt from his hands. "Lost my head. Couldn't help myself." He winced at Sabrina's furious glance. "Sorry! Won't happen again."

She was secretly glad of this crucial assistance, but continued to glower at him as she picked up the tire iron and began fastening the lugs. Within another few minutes the tire was screwed firmly in place. She outdid herself, leaning on the iron to make sure the screws were as tight as they possibly could be, and her fingers were aching, her palms chafed and stinging by the time she got the hubcap back in place. She gave it a last kick after whacking it around the edges with the iron, then began to lower the jack.

"That's not a new tire," Drew said, leaning in to watch

as the back end of the car slowly descended. "Treads look nearly bald."

"I'm sure it'll do," she said from between clenched teeth, each pump of the jack handle seeming to put a groove in her palms.

According to her watch it was well after midnight when they finally got back into the little VW bug. Other than one broken nail, runs in both stockings, grease and dirt all over her aching hands, and the beginnings of a tension headache behind her eyes, Sabrina felt like a million dollars as she turned the key in the ignition. Drew was graceful enough to commend her effusively on her auto-mechanical expertise, and even though she sensed an edge of patronizing humor behind his admiration, she was glad she'd proved her point. She'd gotten the tire fixed without any—well, almost without any—assistance from him, and that accomplishment nearly made the whole disagreeable incident worthwhile.

They pulled back onto the road, Sabrina whistling absently in triumph. She was thinking that she probably looked a mess, and was concentrating on the alluring prospect of a nice hot shower or a leisurely bubble bath.

"Think we need some oil," Drew said conversationally, interrupting Sabrina's reverie. "Or is that little light just for show?"

Sabrina looked at the dashboard. An orange button of light was glowing there, indicating that the oil was, indeed, low. She sighed. The powers that be seemed determined to make this trip back to the city as insufferable as possible. She leaned forward, peering through the windshield. There was an exit coming up.

"We'll turn off here," she announced, praying that there would be a gas station in sight. As they approached the turnoff, she noted thankfully a sign indicating gas and food.

The road off the turnpike was less well lit and only two lanes wide. The wilds of New Jersey appeared to consist of trees, shrubbery, and the occasional industrial building in the dimly discernible distance, but little in the way of civilization. Sabrina drove on, anxiety increasing with each mile as the minutes passed and no gas station appeared.

"The sign said gas and food," she said aloud.

"Yup," he said, then added philosophically, "though you can't believe everything you read these days . . . Hey, I think we're approaching the bustling metropolis of Arcady."

They had passed a rusted sign bearing the town's name, and now some homes and a block of commercial stores, all shut down for the night, appeared on either side of them. The town appeared to contain the bare minimum to qualify it as such, including an inn that looked more like a trailer camp and a cracked neon sign that indicated DANCE AND DRINK.

They were through it as abruptly as they'd entered. Once more desolation reigned, and Sabrina was almost about to give in to full-fledged panic when a gas station sign loomed up ahead.

"Here we go," she said with false brightness.

"Hope it's open," Drew commented.

It wasn't. In fact, the owner was locking up for the night as they pulled into the two-pump station. Sabrina honked. The elderly man at the door to the little garage looked up, shaking his head, and appeared about to walk right off the premises. Sabrina emitted a little moan of consternation. Drew was out of the car in a flash.

She watched him confer with the old man, who never broke his stride, apparently determined to be stubbornly uncooperative. Then Drew stopped him, and by the way the man shook Drew's hand, Sabrina realized that the mystical power of some crisp bills had done the trick. The owner reopened his shop long enough to produce a can of oil.

Drew waved a hand at her impatiently as she moved to get out of the car. "Just open the hood," he called. "You've done enough auto work for the night."

When he'd refilled the oil the little light disappeared, and they pulled out of the station, Sabrina breathing a heavy sigh of relief. It was nearly one in the morning, and she'd begun to feel she was inhabiting a waking nightmare.

"Well," she said as they started back down the country road, "I guess we've had enough adventure for the night."

"It's been great fun," Drew said. She looked at him. He was smiling, apparently sincerely. His hair was tousled from the wind, and with his white teeth gleaming and soft eyes glinting in his tanned, lean face, he was undeniably appealing—spirits still good, humor still intact in spite of the hour and the situation. Sabrina felt a tinge of regret for being as hard on him as she'd been. Many other men she knew would have been terrible company in comparable circumstances. He was at least a good sport.

"Well, car trouble isn't my idea of a good time," she said. "But we seem to be—"

She stopped. Drew noticed it as she did, stiffening, his head cocked to the window. There was a thumping sound that grew louder even as they listened, and Sabrina had to struggle to keep the car from pulling sideways.

"Slow down," Drew said.

"I am."

"Pull over."

Gritting her teeth, Sabrina steered the car off the road. Dirt and gravel rose in the air as they slowed to a halt. She jabbed the handle of her door down, nearly taking it off, and climbed out. Drew's door slammed after hers.

The two of them stood in silence for a long moment, merely staring at the left rear tire she'd labored so hard to put on. Whatever air had been in it a mere fifteen minutes earlier was long gone now.

"I told you it was—"

"Don't say it," she interrupted. "Bald, yes. But did you happen to notice another one in the trunk?"

Drew shook his head. He wasn't smiling now. Sabrina put a hand over her weary eyes and silently cursed, in methodical succession, Lydia, Lydia's husband, New Jersey, Germany, and Henry Ford. When she opened her eyes

Drew was opening the Volkswagen door and taking out his suitbag.

"Going somewhere?"

Drew shrugged. "Well, we know the gas station's hopeless. That guy was on his way home before I had that can of oil open. Something tells me the nearest all-night towing service isn't located behind any of these elm trees. We're gonna have to hoof it."

As they began trudging down the road Sabrina realized how glad she was that she hadn't, at least, worn high heels. Drew yawned loudly at her side. Apparently his long day, and now night, were finally taking a toll.

"Fascinating business, this speaking," he said. "You get to see so many parts of the country you'd never ordinarily—"

"Please," Sabrina interjected. "Don't rub it in."

Drew yawned again. "Seriously," he said, "I did enjoy giving that talk. I think you and Lydia may actually be getting me hooked on public speaking."

"You're good at it," she admitted grudgingly, then yawned herself. She frowned at the endless line of trees and fenceposts, the only scenery on either side of them.

"Getting colder," Drew noted laconically. He shifted his bag from one shoulder to the other.

"Look, I hope you're not blaming me for this," she said crossly. "If you hadn't had to go down to Washington in the first place—"

"Peace," he was saying, waving two spread fingers in the air. "Look—isn't that the edge of Arcady ahead?"

The road was winding into the small town they'd passed earlier. It was ominously silent as they approached; no lights shone from any of the buildings, even the pint-sized combination bar and ballroom having shut down for the night.

"Let's try the Arcady Inn," Drew said. "They've got to have a phone."

It took persistent knocking at the front door of the ramshackle office of the small motel before a light went on inside. At last the door was unlocked and unbolted, and a diminutive gray-haired woman in a bathrobe peered out at them, obviously not predisposed toward friendliness at this late hour.

"Yes?" she said in a cranky, high-pitched voice. "What's the trouble?"

Again Sabrina was grudgingly grateful for Drew's ability to maintain his composure and charm strangers with ease. The woman let them in, sleepily looked up the number of the nearest late-night gas station, and allowed them the use of her phone.

"Poor dear," she addressed Sabrina as Drew talked to someone three towns away. "You're not looking exactly daisy-fresh. Want to use the washroom?"

Sabrina nodded. One look in the mirror of the tiny little bathroom off the office assured her she'd better not look again. She threw some lukewarm water on her face and managed to scrub the worst of the stains on her hands off with powdered soap. She ran a brush through her disheveled hair, and then, feeling and looking slightly more human, emerged.

The elderly woman was leaning on the counter, her chin propped up in her palms, watching Drew sign something with a pen that was chained to the top. She turned to smile at Sabrina.

"Well, Mrs. Dalton, you're in luck."

Sabrina stopped in her tracks. "Excuse me?"

Drew turned around to face her. "Well, hon," he said, a certain malicious pleasure in this charade evident on his smiling face. "The fellows over at A and O Olsen Esso have their hands full with an accident down the turnpike. They won't be able to pick up our car until morning. But Mrs. Josefs here has one room vacant tonight, and she's willing to put us up for a mere pittance. Isn't that something?"

"A room?" Sabrina bit her lip nervously.

"Shower and color TV," said Mrs. Josefs with a certain pride.

Sabrina looked at Drew. "Maybe we should walk back..."

Mrs. Josefs's eyes widened. "She's overtired," Drew said, placating the woman. He walked quickly up to Sabrina and guided her gently but firmly to the door, safely out of the motel owner's earshot. "You could walk," he said pleasantly. "Maybe you could rustle up a taxi service in some other town, though I doubt it, and be fleeced of a small fortune to get back to Manhattan by sun-up. But I'm beat," he continued quietly. "If you're worried about keeping your virtue intact, let me assure you—I have nothing but sleep on my mind."

Sabrina stared at him, her exhausted brain hopelessly circling in search of an alternative. He was right, of course. She noted the red in his eyes and took stock of her own head-to-foot weariness.

"I should have brought the tire iron," she said, hiding a grin. "To make sure you keep your distance."

Drew smiled. "Lady, you could knock me out with a feather. Let's check in."

The room was tiny. A frayed and worn carpet of some dismally indistinguishable color stretched from wall to paper-peeling wall. For a moment they both stood in the doorway surveying the uninviting interior, with the requisite wildlife painting over an incongruously large TV set, the frilly curtained window, the one grotesque imitation antique chair—and the bed. The bed was not king-size, not queen-size, but a dubious double. Perfect for one person who liked to stretch out, perhaps, or a couple much more intimately acquainted than they.

"I'd carry you across the threshold, darling, but I've got this suitbag..."

"Quite all right," said Sabrina, stalking resolutely into the room. There wasn't all that far to go. Its dimensions were so tiny that only a few steps brought her right up to the foot of the bed. She turned, and then sat on the edge of it, not knowing what else to do. Drew closed the door behind them and crossed to the little bedside lamp, its base a glazed green clay leprechaun figurine that was no doubt an escapee from a Jersey flea market. The light flicked on, and Drew turned off the overhead, which dispelled slightly the vividly squalid atmosphere.

Sabrina was suddenly wide awake. She sat stiffly, not moving, her bag perched rather primly on her knees. Drew, having located the closet, opened it, hung his suitbag within, and was then unable to slide the door completely shut. He wrestled with it a moment, then gave up, putting his arms up in the air and leaning back, stretching. Looking at her, he put a hand over his mouth as a huge yawn overtook him. "You're not hungry, are you?"

Sabrina shook her head.

"Me neither." He took his jacket off and draped it over the chair, then stood by the television, silently deliberating.

"Well," he said, flipping it on and hastily turning down the volume. "I'm going to sit right here"—he sat down on the bed, which creaked unmercifully, and faced the flickering screen—"and see what's on for a few minutes. You can pretend I'm not even here."

His back was pointedly to her. It took Sabrina a moment to fully comprehend what was an understatedly gallant gesture on Drew's part. Then she got up quickly. The bed groaned again in protest.

"I'll just use the..." she murmured. Drew remained, absorption real or feigned, silently watching the tube. She entered the tiny, chilly bathroom, clutching her bag, and shut the door. In gray-blue fluorescent light she looked even more pale and harried than she'd imagined she did. Sabrina rolled off the ruined panty hose. For no logical reason she stuffed them into her bag, then paused uncertainly.

Her heart was pounding at an unnaturally fast rate. Her palms felt a bit sweaty. Sabrina realized she felt about as keyed-up and nervous as a high schooler on prom night. Get a grip, she told the face in the mirror. Biding time, she combed her hair and buttoned up her cardigan. Her skirt would keep her legs fairly warm, she decided. Wearing her overcoat to bed was absurd, but she wasn't shedding another thing. Not with *him*—and the thought gave her insides a little tug—in a bed that small.

When she emerged from the bathroom Drew was still facing the TV. Sabrina stood at the opposite side of the bed, momentarily indecisive. Then she grabbed the top edge of the bed's coverlet—one of those white, imitation-cotton jobs festooned with little balls of fluff—and pulled it down below the pillow on her side. She lifted the edge of the covers, yanking loose the folded edge of the tightly tucked sheet, and then gingerly slid into the bed.

The springs sang, the headboard rattled against the wall, and the entire contraption emitted a small symphony of creaks, pops, and thumps as she eased her legs between the ice-cold sheets. Drew rose from his side of the bed and flipped off the TV.

"Insomniac's special," he nodded, indicating the bed.

"Do you think we can get more heat in here?" Sabrina asked.

Drew looked down at her, a flicker of amusement crossing his face. "I'm sure we could," he said slowly. "But I'll see if there's a thermostat."

Sabrina watched him, silent, the covers pulled up to just below her chin, as he located the little rheostat on the wall by the door and fiddled with it. There was a rumble and a muffled rush of air from the wall heater near her side of the bed.

"Thanks," she called. Drew nodded. He returned to his side of the bed and flicked off the leprechaun lamp. The room was plunged into darkness. As her eyes became adjusted to the light, Sabrina vaguely made out Drew's form nearby and heard the sounds of his shirt being unbuttoned, the rattle of his belt buckle. The intimate noise of his zipper brought vividly to mind her earlier encounter with Drew in his dressing room.

But now he was removing his trousers. Sabrina realized she was clutching the covers to her so tightly that he wouldn't be able to get into the bed. Maybe that was the best idea. Well, what had she expected? That he sleep, fully clothed, on the floor?

His hands tugged on the sheet. Sabrina slowly unclenched her hands. Surely she was being ridiculous. She was a grown woman, and he a grown man . . . which, come to think of it, was exactly the problem. As the bed began squealing and moaning beneath Drew's impending weight, Sabrina quickly wriggled to the right, trying to put a minimal inch or two between her body and his.

Even once Drew was settled beside her on his back, the bed continued to sway slightly, the springs quietly wheezing. Any shifting about or motion at all, she soon discovered, provoked a noise completely disproportionate to its cause. As she turned on her side, so that her back would be to Drew. a loud metallic rasp sounded from directly beneath her.

"Good night, dear wife," Drew said congenially. Even without seeing his face, Sabrina could imagine the impish grin that was no doubt punctuating this salutation.

"'Night," she muttered, and tried once more to put some space between them. This turned out to be harder than she'd suspected. The bed had a definite dip in the middle, and the sides sloped toward it, so Sabrina had to actually take hold of the edge of the mattress and keep her body forcibly suspended in a position that was annoyingly uncomfortable to avoid contact with his.

After a few minutes she decided this approach was untenable. Ever so slowly, a millimeter at a time, she relaxed her grip on the mattress side, and let her body's weight naturally lean with the slope of the bed. Inch by inch her back moved toward the bed's center. When it encountered the very edge of Drew's arm and shoulder, she froze, and then, hearing his soft breathing appear even and unperturbed, she relaxed gradually, allowing herself to slowly slide into position against his length.

From the sound of it, sleep was coming very easily to her companion, but for Sabrina it seemed like an absolute impossibility. All her senses were unnaturally acute. She could hear every rustle of wind, see every pattern on the wallpaper a few feet from her face, feel every contour of Drew's inert body against hers, and smell the faint but sharply sweet, pungent scent of his after shave. As she listened to the sounds of the night, forcing her eyes shut, she reflected that it had been quite some time since she had last shared a bed with a man. It was almost comforting, in an odd way, but whatever sense of security she might have garnered from this experience was being overpowered by the anxiety, the restlessness, the . . . oh, all right!—arousal, she felt, knowing the identity of the more-than-stranger and less-than-friend whose body was casually resting against hers.

A flushing noise accompanied by gurgling pipes shattered the silence, seemingly so close that she twitched involuntarily, and the bed squeaked. The walls were obviously paper-thin. She could hear each footstep of the next room's occupant. There was one click—a light switch?—then another. Television? At two in the morning?

Sabrina sighed. A distant, subdued din of gunfire and horses' hooves sounded directly behind the headboard. The late-night-western fan next door was the last straw. She might as well count spots on the ceiling. Carefully, trying to provoke only a minimal plethora of jangles, squeaks, and rattles, Sabrina turned onto her back.

She stole a glance at Drew. In the darkness she could just discern his profile. His handsome face appeared serene in repose. She admired, reluctantly, the strong line of his high forehead, aquiline nose, the slightly parted lips, the jutting chin. One naked arm was slung over his half-covered chest. She watched the slow rise and fall of the dark hair, the strong, finely molded musculature of his upper arms and shoulders gleaming softly in the pale light from a lone streetlamp outside the shaded window.

A curly tendril of black hair had fallen over his left eyebrow, almost touching the long-lashed lid. She was seized with a sudden, unconscionable urge to smooth the lock of hair back from his face, but stifled the impulse. Their next-door neighbor was changing channels now. The subdued babble of an advertisement floated through the wall.

Drew's eyes flickered open. "Of all the motels in all the towns in all the states of America, he walks into ours," he said wryly in a voice slightly raspy with sleep. He turned his head to look at her, and smiled.

She smiled back. And then his smile widened. And a giggle at the absurdity of their position bubbled up in her throat. Then they were laughing, both of them, and the answering squeals and rattles from the bed only provoked more laughter from them, their bodies shaking with uncontrollable gales as the springs and frame virtually thundered beneath them.

At last their laughter subsided. As she faced him, seeing the slow ebbing of her own helpless hysteria mirrored in the crinkles beside his eyes, it seemed only natural that his hand reached out to smooth the hair back from her cheek. It seemed only intuitive that her body turn to his, only fitting that his face slide closer to hers across the pillow. And when his lips closed gently, tenderly affectionate, over hers, she had the sense that a long-awaited, inevitable moment had arrived.

His clean, musky scent enveloped her as his hand caressed her cheek softly and his lips parted hers soundlessly. His tongue made a gentle tour of the moist recesses of her mouth, and her tongue extended to meet his. She tasted the sweetness of his kiss, moving without thought, the space that had been between them now an annoying barrier. Her arm rose from under his, her hand sliding over his warm, naked skin as his arms cradled her in a breathless embrace.

He pulled her close, his tongue more urgently caressing hers. His fingers were tangled now in the silken strands of her hair. As her hands roamed over his smooth warm skin she could feel his muscles rippling. Slowly he lifted his lips from hers. His warm breath mingled with her own as his eyes probed deeply into hers.

"God, how I want you," he murmured.

"Drew," she said weakly. "Don't—"

But her words died as his lips found the soft hollow of her neck, and he traced an exquisite, fiery trail of kisses down her quivering skin. His fingers deftly unbuttoned her sweater, clearing a path for his hungry mouth. A moan escaped her in a deep shuddering breath as his hand cupped one breast, aching and straining with arousal beneath the lacy encasement of her brassiere. Then his lips were joined with hers again. Her hands grasped him tightly, her fingers running through the thick softness of his hair, her body beginning a slow undulation against his that was instinctive, uncontrollable.

Even though his caresses seemed teasingly, tantalizingly restrained, she could feel the mounting urgency of his desire matching her own. But as his fingers found the front clasp of her bra and twisted it undone, an undercurrent of fearful foreboding seeped into her awareness. What was she doing— letting him do? How could she surrender like this when she should have been fighting him off?

Then his soft strong hand closed over the mound of her naked breast and she gasped, the dark nipple hardening in his palm. Her own hands slid down his broad back as a molten fire of nearly painful intensity surged from the depths of her at his continued caress. She struggled to free herself from the erotic haze his touch provoked, aware that in a moment there would be no turning back.

She was tempted to let go, to go with him to the pinnacle of pleasure she was already glimpsing within reach. But the very intensity of her arousal was alarming her. Fear of losing control, of surrendering all her power to his, slowed her response to Drew's caresses. She hovered, the passion arrested, in his grasp, sensing that Drew was...listening to her, somehow, with hands and lips, waiting for her intensity to match his own.

She was aware, again, of the symphony of squeaks and squealings, the rhythmic sighing of the springs beneath them, the counterpoint of the television in the next room. The ceiling, with its patterns of cracks and discolorations, swam into view. More strongly now, she felt a stab of self-consciousness at her wild abandonment to this man she hardly knew, and at the absurd seaminess of their surroundings.

Drew lifted his face from the tangle of her hair, his eyes glowing, questioningly gazing into hers in the darkness. Had he felt the sudden stiffening in her body, sensed the discomfort that suffused her?

"Sabrina," he said softly, his voice a throaty rasp of desire.

She gazed up at him, mute. Even though moments before she had felt the stirrings of a budding trust in him, had felt her whole being rise to life beneath the magical ministrations of his hands, he looked oddly unfamiliar to her now.

She felt her cheeks flush as Drew's eyes explored hers. She felt trapped beneath him, pinned beneath his probing gaze. Her vulnerability was excruciatingly embarrassing to her, lying half-naked underneath him, her breath still heavy with arousal.

"Sabrina, you're the most beautiful woman..." He shook his head, his hand tenderly smoothing a tendril of hair from her cheek. His voice was a husky caress. "And you and I are going to have the most beautiful experience"—he paused, a sensuous smile playing at the corners of his mouth—"but not here, sweetheart—not now. Not like this."

Another round of gunfire from the TV next door and a whirring metallic noise from the heater seemed to underline his words.

"Holding myself back from loving you the way I want

to borders on torture," he said softly, and as he shifted his weight, his thighs sliding over hers, she could feel the taut evidence of his arousal. "But you deserve more than this, Sabrina. *We* do. I told you we were having a romance—and this is more like a scene from a sordid affair."

Sabrina exhaled slowly. Although she felt a twinge of annoyance at his typically masterful control of the situation, she was grateful for his sensitivity—and for the chance to come to her senses. "Or a scene from a western," she murmured, modestly pulling her sweater closed as thundering hooves and Indian whoops sounded behind them.

Drew chuckled. He bent down to kiss her again, but she pulled away from him, the bed beginning a noisy chorus of protest. "Next time," he began, "I'll take you—"

"Whoa, pardner," she said quickly, turning her shoulder and fastening her bra. "This time was too much for me, to begin with," she went on, buttoning up her sweater with shaky hands. "I don't know what got into me. I was being consummately unprofessional."

"You were being a woman," he said softly. "A gorgeously passionate woman, I might add."

"Well, I'm glad you're being a gentleman," she said, stiffening as his hand settled over her shoulder. "Please, Drew—don't. We really should just go to sleep."

He squeezed her shoulder gently, then withdrew his hand. "All right," he said simply. "But there's no reason to regret—"

"Good night, Drew," she said before he could continue. Chagrined at having nearly lost her head and given herself over to him, she wanted no more conversation. She huddled herself as far from him as she could, resolutely turned away with her head burrowed into the thin motel pillow.

Behind her, Drew lay back. "Sweet dreams, Sabrina," he said when the bed's wheezings and wailings had quieted.

Fat chance, she silently replied.

In the stillness of the room her heartbeat still sounded loud in her ears. That had been close, too close. Wide-eyed in the darkness, she listened to his breathing. At last the strains of a patriotic hymn that signaled the station's sign-off drifted through the wall, and she heard a gentle snore from Drew. Sabrina shut her eyes and prayed for sleep to come.

7

"AAAAAH . . . AH—"

"Bless you."

"—choo!" Sabrina brought the handkerchief to her reddened nose, momentarily covering the receiver.

"Are you drinking fluids?" Lydia was saying.

"Plenty." Sabrina sniffled.

"Don't come in tomorrow," Lydia said. "You sound like
hell."

"Feel like it, too," she said, pulling her bathrobe tighter.
She smiled though. Lydia usually expected her to come in,
come hell or high water. But for once her boss was feeling
guilty. Blame for the bald spare tire had fallen squarely on
Lydia, who, come to think of it, did remember now that
Henry had warned her he hadn't had time to get a new one
in the car after their last flat, and she was obviously trying
to make amends.

The cold had come upon her not long after waking up in that wretched motel room early Saturday morning. Probably being overtired from little sleep and then hanging around on a chilly New Jersey backroad shortly after sun-up while a local mechanic put a new tire on the car had done the trick. By the time she'd dropped Drew at his place she was sneezing at regular intervals, prompting him to surmise, wryly, that she was now allergic to him.

She didn't disagree, though she secretly wished that she were. She wished she had something stronger than her obviously weakened power of resistance with which to counteract Drew's effect on her. That morning, when she'd woken to peer through the half-opened bathroom door, catching sight of Drew shaving—shirtless—she'd been seized with a compulsive urge to rise from the bed and run her hands down that manly back of his. She hadn't, of course, but had he tried to seduce her then, she might well have succumbed.

Fortunately he had been intent only on getting them back to the city, and hadn't referred to the events of the night. As Sabrina gradually wakened she, too, had acted as if nothing unusual had taken place; had done nothing to indicate she had very nearly been carried away by his shiver-provoking caresses, had nearly lost all control in the simmering heat of his embrace...

But a different sort of hot shiver suffused her as the day went on. By Saturday night, having returned the car to Lydia and taxied back to her place to crawl immediately under her covers, she had a full-fledged fever. Sunday morning she felt appreciably better, the cold now lodged firmly in her swollen nose, but if Lydia was offering a day off, she wasn't going to refuse.

"I'll take the morning off at any rate," she told her.

"Fine," said Lydia. "So other than that, Mrs. Lincoln, how did you enjoy the show?"

"Like I told you, everything was fine."

"You were too busy sneezing yesterday to give me *all*

the lurid details. You left out, for example, a review of your night at the inn."

"Some inn," said Sabrina. "It was more like a...ah ...ahhhh—"

"Bless you."

"—choo! I wish you wouldn't do that," she said crossly, gingerly patting her nose with the handkerchief.

"Do what?"

"Say bless you before I've actually sneezed."

"You *do* need some rest, dear," Lydia said. "I'll call you tomorrow."

No sooner had she hung up the phone than it rang again. "What did you forget?" Sabrina asked.

"I haven't forgotten a single moment, actually," Drew said, the warm, husky resonance of his voice momentarily startling her into silence. "Hello? Sabrina?"

"She's not here," Sabrina said.

He chuckled. "Twin sister?"

Sabrina sighed. "I've got a cold. I'm even less capable of carrying on a civil conversation now than when I saw you last. What do you want?"

"Well, I wanted to see how you were," he began.

"Got the picture?"

"I guess so," he said, unperturbed. "Need anything?"

"Solitude," she said pointedly.

"Drinking liquids? Taking vitamins?"

"Yes, Dr. Dalton." She sighed. "Look, I really can't talk. Thanks for being a sport about everything, you know, with the car and all. I've got—ah—to—aaah..."

"Bless you."

"—choo!" Her head was throbbing. "Good grief," she said, sniffing. "New Yorkers don't even let you sneeze right!"

"Excuse me?"

"You guys are all too fast on the draw," she said.

"You sound terrible," he added. "How will I be sure you're getting plenty of rest?"

"You know, Dalton, I don't understand you at all," she said irritably. "You didn't seem to care whether I lived or died a week or so ago, and now that I have a common cold I can't get rid of you. Why is that?"

"Ah," he said. "So Plan B did have some effect."

"Plan B?"

"I decided that if my persistent attention was rubbing you the wrong way, I'd give you a little breathing room. So you missed me, did you?"

"No!" she said vehemently. "I noticed you weren't bothering me for a while, that's all. It was quite . . . qui—ah . . ." She paused to sneeze.

"Gesundheit," Drew said, after allowing her time for a proper full-length sneeze.

"It was quite pleasant," she finished.

"Not so pleasant for me," Drew said. "It was difficult, not . . . bothering you."

"I'm sure you had other things to do." She sniffled.

"I did," he said. "For example, I terminated a couple of relationships that had once looked promising, pre-you."

"Pre-me? What do you mean?"

"I've cleared the decks, so to speak. From now on I'm absolutely free and clear to devote my romantic attentions entirely to you."

"You *are* crazy," she said, incredulous. "Look, whoever you—ah, terminated, you'd better reactivate! I've told you once, twice, and finally, now—I'm not interested in seeing you! I don't want to be involved at all! Whatever's going on between us so far has been pure fiasco, as far as—as— aah . . ." With this sneeze her head began to pound in earnest.

"I think you're overreacting," he said mildly.

"Overre—" She winced, putting her fingers to her throbbing temple. "You're overestimating your charm, that's the problem! I don't want to see you; I don't want to talk to you—"

"I know you don't mean that," he said calmly.

"You—" Words failed her. With a groan of exasperation she slammed the receiver down. After a moment's thought she disconnected the telephone.

She spent the rest of her weekend doing all the proper and necessary things to hasten recovery, and by Monday morning the cold had dwindled to a mere lingering sniffle. A bad case of cabin fever had struck her, however, rising in inverse proportion to the abating bug. By noon, unable to spend another minute in her cramped apartment, Sabrina bundled herself up and headed out to work.

The air was crisp, with a hint of the oncoming winter. She welcomed the bustling atmosphere of the Upper West Side. The brilliant sun cut through the chill, and when the crosstown bus seemed too long in coming for her impatient spirits, jittery from being cooped up, she wrapped her long woolen muffler securely about her and headed for the park on foot. The bus caught up with her just before Central Park West, so she hopped aboard then, and was soon walking down the block to her office.

Sunlight glinted blindingly off the windows of Drew Dalton's little castle in the sky as she looked up. Sabrina averted her eyes. Perhaps she'd finally succeeded in scaring him off. Maybe by now he sensed she was more trouble than he'd bargained for. After the way she'd acted, he surely knew she wasn't the easy, casual conquest she was probably used to. Doubtless he was already looking elsewhere for romance.

The thought of being freed from Drew's attentions should have cheered her. But she felt depressed as she took the elevator upstairs. So the unexpectedly celebratory atmosphere at the office caught her completely unprepared.

She knew something was up the moment she walked through the door. The phones were ringing and the whole office was alive with the babble of voices. Lucy was temporarily ensconced at her desk, talking on the phone. She waved a sheaf of messages excitedly at Sabrina in greeting.

Carrie was talking on her line, with another call on hold, beaming with unusual intensity. Lydia had two cigarettes lit, one in her hand and one in her ashtray, and she was standing by her desk, phone in hand, gesturing wildly for Sabrina to look at something while she continued talking in a subdued, businesslike manner to what sounded like an interested new client.

Sabrina took the magazine Lydia handed her, and was momentarily unnerved to see a glossy black-and-white smiling Drew Dalton on the opened page. "I've been trying to reach you all morning," Lydia hissed, her hand cupped over the receiver. "Where were you?"

"I was . . . Oh!" she said, suddenly remembering. "I disconnected the phone. What's this all—"

Lydia waved her silent, returning to her conversation, and merely mouthed the word *read* at her, tapping the magazine page. Sabrina sat in the chair by the desk, unwinding her scarf. It was the latest issue of *Personality*. She glanced at the by-line. So, Kay Cristy had finally gotten her story after all. Sabrina quickly scanned the opening paragraphs, a rehash of Drew's achievements, and continued skimming, beginning to wonder what the fuss was all about. A page later she sat bolt upright.

CELEBRITY SPEAKING—BIG BUCKS FOR THE BIG NAMES read the headline of a separate column, and her eye was immediately drawn to a smaller box at the bottom of the page, where the name EVANS SPEAKERS in boldface type jumped out at her. Her heartbeat accelerating, Sabrina read the paragraph.

Of the many agencies handling celebrity speakers in entertainment and business, Dalton chose Evans Speakers to represent him, a surprising choice, as it's a relatively small bureau run by, and representing almost exclusively, women—columnist Nan Flanders, TV anchorwoman Vanessa Brown, and best-selling author Trish Haywood are among those heading their roster. Why Evans? "They're smart ladies," says Dalton. "They know what they're doing. And I'd rather be handled by a small company that gives me intensified personal attention than be lost in the shuffle at a large agency like Sprint's." It's unlikely that Dalton, who commands a whopping $15,000 plus expenses for each appearance, would be ignored at any speaker bureau—but his endorsement of Evans is certainly making this bureau a name to be reckoned with.

Of the more established agencies, Harry Sprint is perhaps most popular among big names on the circuit . . .

The article went on to cite other agencies in the field. Sabrina realized that only in the context of an article about Drew would their name be given such attention—it was the kind of national publicity one couldn't even buy, and it had obviously generated an immediate response. She looked up, excitement rising in her fast.

"It hit the newsstands Saturday," Lydia said, hanging up. "We had a hundred and thirty-two messages on the service this morning."

"Phil Harris on oh-two, Lydia." Carrie's voice competed with Lucy's, who had a call for her as well.

"Hold all calls for three minutes," Lydia yelled. "I'm in conference with my junior partner!" She shut the door and turned to face Sabrina, the sparkle in her eyes magnified by her glasses. "This is it, cookie," she said, grabbing her hand and squeezing it. "We're about to start playing hardball with the big boys."

Sabrina squeezed back, aware that she was smiling dumbly. "Who—how many—what have we—"

"People we couldn't get past secretaries to talk to are calling up personally," Lydia said, lighting a cigarette. "Newmark. Holt. That guy from *Live at Six*. We've got them coming from both sides—dozens of meeting planners, convention heads. What do you think?"

"I think it's unbelievable," Sabrina said. "I just wish..."

"They'd gotten the name right?" Lydia nodded. "It's okay."

"He did it," Sabrina said, struck suddenly by the thought.

"He certainly did. At the moment we've got more business than we—"

"No, I mean he did it, on purpose," she interrupted, annoyed. "Drew must have told them we were Evans Speakers—he was on my case to drop the Resources just the other day."

"Well, I'll admit I was little peeved when I noticed it, but..." Lydia shrugged. "They spelled Evans right, and that's what matters."

"It's the principle," Sabrina frowned.

"It *is* a cleaner name," Lydia mused. "And we'll be able to afford new stationery soon enough if we want to go with it. Sabrina!" She lifted Sabrina's chin with her hand. "Why do you want to rain on your own parade? Dear, it's not important."

"You're right." Sabrina smiled. "Well! I guess I should start manning a phone." She indicated the magazine. "Got another copy?"

"Sure. I had Carrie buy a half dozen. We'll want to get a blowup, reprint, whatever-you-call-it—for the mailings."

Sabrina nodded, taking the magazine. "Any other mentions?"

A shadow of vague distress flittered across Lydia's face, then vanished. "Oh, there's one passing comment in the interview, but I don't think it's usable for publicity."

Sabrina paused at the door. "Why?"

"Well, it's an annoying crack he made—not important really, but a little...patronizing."

"Really?" Sabrina reopened the copy she was holding.

"Nothing to worry about, dear." Lydia opened the door. "Let's go out later and celebrate—what do you say?"

"Sure," Sabrina said, already preoccupied in rereading

the article on Drew from the beginning.

"All right, Carrie, bring 'em on!" Lydia called. "Sabrina can start taking some of the calls now, too. Check with me," she told Sabrina, "before you schedule appointments. I've got a full week's worth already."

Sabrina nodded. Lucy vacated her desk as she came in. "Receiver's warm," she told Sabrina, exiting. "Have fun."

Sabrina sat down at her desk, too absorbed in the article to bother taking off her coat. After the opening descriptive paragraphs, there was a two-page interview prepared with occasional commentary by the journalist. Midway through the second page, Sabrina found the passage Lydia had undoubtedly been referring to.

DALTON: Of course, success can breed success.
PERSONALITY: So it would seem, judging by your own example. Your recent endorsement of the Jove computer put that fledgling company on the map. By signing with Evans Speakers, you've singlehandedly legitimized what had been a fairly obscure agency that handled only women.
DALTON: They were doing all right, for women—but yes, they needed me to develop their success potential.
PERSONALITY: That's a term you devote a chapter to in your book. Can you elaborate briefly on the concept of "success potential"?

Sabrina read it once, twice, then comprehended suddenly what it really meant to see red as the magazine page dissolved before her eyes and the searing heat of furious indignation rose inside her. The magazine clutched in her hand, she marched back into Lydia's office.

Lydia was absorbed in another phone call with a prospective client. She looked, saw Sabrina's flaring nostrils, winced, then shrugged helplessly, pantomiming that they would talk later.

"Who does that asinine, arrogant, balloon-headed reptile think he is?" she stormed.

Lydia clapped a hand over her phone. "Would you kindly——" she said witheringly.

"So he's singlehandedly legitimized us, has he? I'd like to singlehandedly knock his——all right, all right!" she hissed as Lydia silently shushed her. Sabrina turned abruptly and stalked out of the office. Then, without breaking stride, she continued onward, past a startled Carrie, and headed for the elevator, slamming the door behind her.

She read the paragraph again as the elevator descended. "Doing all right——for women," she muttered through clenched teeth, and she marched out of the elevator, flinging one end of her woolen scarf over her shoulder.

The doorman in Drew's building across the street was absorbed in talking on the intercom as a messenger waited. Sabrina was past him so fast, he barely had time to register her whirlwind appearance.

"Hey, lady," he called as she punched the elevator buzzer down the entrance hall with her fist. "You can't——"

"I can too," she snarled. The door slid open, and she quickly jabbed the Penthouse button. She was on her way up before the doorman could interfere, the *Personality* issue by now grasped tightly in her hand, rolled up like a club.

The elevator stopped on the top floor. Her momentum was briefly slowed when the door opened right onto one end of what appeared to be the penthouse's living room. She was momentarily dazzled by the sun-filled expanse of gleaming blond hardwood floors, off-white walls and columns, and huge windows on every wall. Her eyes swept the airy, open room flooded with light, registering elegantly modernistic chairs and low-slung black glass tables on a finely woven rug of pastel geometric shapes, the tastefully upholstered banquette lining one wall by a built-in fireplace. Seated in a little dining room alcove, his hair highlighted by the sun streaming through the skylight windows above him, Drew Dalton sat in a flannel shirt open above dark jeans, a sheaf of papers on the blond wood table before him. His coffee cup suspended between the saucer and his lips, he looked at Sabrina, frozen in surprise.

Sabrina set her lips tightly together and stalked across the room as the elevator shut quietly behind her. As Drew watched her approach, expressionless, her anger grew. Reaching the table, towering above him for once, she raised the rolled magazine, sorely tempted to bring it down right on the crown of his carefully combed head. Instead, she slammed the offensive issue on the tabletop, rattling his saucer and scattering some papers.

"You're a swine, Dalton. Pomposity on the podium is one thing, but I'd appreciate your not slandering us in print to service your ghastly swollen ego!"

Drew raised one eyebrow. "Pardon?" he said amicably.

"Don't be cute. I suppose you've seen this?" She brandished the magazine in his face.

He took it from her and glanced at the offending page. "I saw an early draft," he said mildly. "What's the matter with it?"

Sabrina exhaled sharply, exasperated. She tapped a forefinger at the paragraph discussing Evans. Drew scanned it, frowning, then looked up at Sabrina, whose arms were folded and eyes were blazing.

"It's been edited slightly," he observed. "There was more to it originally."

"I'm sure," she said. "There was also more to our company's name originally."

A flicker of mischievous amusement appeared in Drew's eyes, then faded. "No, really, I quarreled with the interviewer's characterization of Evans, myself—but the editor obviously deleted that part of our conversation. And I'm not at all sure I ever said that about...doing all right—for women. In fact—"

"I'm supposed to believe that?"

Drew shrugged. "It's true." He looked at Sabrina, who was still trembling with barely contained fury. "Coffee?"

"No!" she shouted. "Look, we were in business long before I met you—"

"I know."

"—successfully in business before we ever met, a day I'm beginning to rue, and I resent—"

"Take it easy."

"—your cavalierly taking the credit for launching us into legitimacy, as if a bureau for women speakers couldn't possibly be as credible—"

"I'm sorry it came out that way."

"—as a men's speaker bureau! For your information, there are just as many successful, legitimate women in business that we've been handling—"

"I know."

"—for quite some time that can command the fees you do! *They* didn't need you to patronize them in print, and *we* don't need you—"

"I said, I'm sorry."

"—to be the big man who gave us the seal of approval! *I* didn't ask for your help, because I don't need your help—"

"Sit down!" Drew barked, and taking hold of Sabrina's shoulder, he shoved her into the seat opposite him. She sat there, glaring at him, catching her breath, and he glowered back. "Now, hold it right there," he said quickly, taking advantage of Sabrina's momentary shock at being manhandled to get a word in. "I've said I'm sorry that the interview as printed has a mildly deprecating characterization in it—"

"More like character assassination," she muttered.

"—but shouldn't you be across the street answering your phone? I know what the circulation of *Personality* is, and unless I'm mistaken, which I doubt, this article should have already generated an interest in you that any businessperson in their right mind would be grateful for."

"Thank you, gracious sovereign," she said sardonically. "I'll just return to the peons' quarters—"

She attempted to get up, but Drew's hand came down over her wrist in an iron grip. "Grow up," he said tersely. "Maybe you didn't ask for any help, but you got it. Why can't you just accept it gracefully instead of storming in here like some sort of she-demon with a vendetta against any man who takes an interest in her?"

"Because I'm not interested in your interest!" she cried. "Nor your insults!"

"Why don't you own up to your feelings, Sabrina? It's no crime to have them. Why are you fighting me—and yourself?"

"Let me go!" she cried, wrenching her arm free. "I don't know what you're talking about." She rose to go, but Drew got up simultaneously and barred her way.

"Yes, you do," he said, and the smoldering intensity of his gaze was frightening. Her heart pounding, she tried to step past him, but he grabbed her, a hand on each arm.

"I don't," she gasped, his powerful hands holding her in place. The look in his eyes was riveting her as well, and she was powerless to move away as his face bent to hers. "Let me—"

Then his lips covered hers. He grasped her wrists, pulling her hands out to bring her body full up against his as his mouth plundered the hidden riches of hers hungrily. The force of his swooping kiss sent her head back, rendering her breathless. Her wide-open eyes glazed suddenly, involuntarily shutting as the delicious assault of his tongue and lips overtook all thought, all other sensation.

She'd balled her hands into fists as she'd strained to pull away. But now her palms opened in a mute gesture of surrender and her body relaxed, then shivered in his grip. Her own tongue sought his with a matching intensity of arousal.

His hands slid slowly up her arms to her shoulders as their kiss deepened, grew wilder in its savage sweetness. He was nudging her coat from her shoulders. It slipped off, fell to the floor as she brought her hands away from his then up around his neck. His hands tightened on her back as he pulled her closer to him, holding her body against his so she could feel the beating of his heart. It raced as fast as hers.

His mouth left hers for a moment, trailing fiery kisses across her cheek, then down the curve of her jaw to her neck, and Sabrina exhaled a shuddery breath as his lips nudged and nuzzled the length of her throat. He lifted his head suddenly then, and the look of luminous intensity she saw as his gaze bored into her eyes made her feel a rush of liquid heat rise from her depths. Now it was she who resumed their kiss, opening her mouth wider, her hands raking through the thickness of his hair.

One of his hands slipped down over her hip, molding it to his, then traveled over her buttocks, up her waist, slipping between their bodies to at last cup her breast beneath her crepe blouse. Again she felt the hot, unfurling excitement within her as his thumb sought the hardening tip, but this time she had no resistance left. She shivered with anticipation, biting the edge of his ear, her face buried in his cheek and neck as he quickly unbuttoned her blouse and, with trembling fingers, unclasped her bra. When his hand closed over the warm vibrant naked skin, she arched her back, gasping with pleasure as his thumb and forefinger teased and fondled the stiffened nipple.

Then both his hands cupped and molded her quivering flesh. He moaned, kissing her again, kissing her neck, descending, his lips searing a path between the cleft of her breasts. His mouth closed on one swollen tip and she cried out, her hands convulsively clutching his neck as she leaned back against the table's edge.

His mouth moved upward to the hollow of her throat, and then he took her mouth again fiercely, urgently. She could feel the hardness of his arousal against her as his hips melded to hers. For a moment Sabrina felt a jolt of apprehensive fear.

"Wait," she breathed weakly. "We can't..."

"We can," he said, his voice a rasp of desire. "The only thing we can't do now is wait."

With that his arm grasped her tightly around the waist. Drew bent down and then, in a single motion, lifted her into the air.

"Put me down!" she cried.

"Soon enough," he said.

As a tumult of conflicting emotions coursed through her captive body, he held her tightly against him, carrying her toward what could only be his bedroom.

"What are you doing?"

He smiled as he maneuvered her through a narrow doorway. "You know what I'm doing," he said.

"But I don't like it!" Her voice was unnaturally tremulous.

"You'll love it," he answered.

"Let me go," she gasped, struggling in his grasp.

"All right."

She was falling suddenly, and even though the bed was soft beneath her, the wind was knocked out of her. Before she could struggle upright, he was on the bed. Even as she moved to escape, his powerful embrace imprisoned her. And as his lips claimed hers again, her last vestiges of resistance were consumed by the fiery lust he loosed within her.

Soon his hands and lips coaxed her into a state of trembling arousal. Every nerve in her skin seemed to pulse in excitement as his body pressed urgently against her flesh. Her own body began to move in an instinctive, primitive rhythm. When he began unbuttoning the rest of her buttons her hands flew to do the same, swiftly undoing the buttons of his shirt, her trembling fingers pausing just to slide through the soft curly hair of his chest.

Only when he had slipped her skirt from her, and his hands slid beneath the waistband of her panty hose, beginning to push them down over her hips, did she tense again, her hands pushing against his shoulders.

"No, stop," she pleaded in a hoarse whisper.

"It's too late to stop," he murmured. Then his mouth followed the course of his hands, and he was right—there was no stopping now.

Her entire body shook as he kissed his way down the length of her nakedness. She moaned as he paused short of pleasuring her fully, but teased and tantalized every inch of her skin into vibrant life. Through a swooning haze of exquisitely torturous arousal, she watched him unbuckle his belt and helped him remove the last of his own clothing with shaky hands.

The first sight of his magnificently toned and sculpted body added a sense of awe to her arousal. He was beautiful unclothed—the broad shoulders and chest tapering to narrow hips, long legs, skin tanned and gleaming. And somehow, in his eyes, as he explored her naked body, his gaze caressing her from head to foot, she saw that awe reflected, and the embarrassment she had felt dissolved.

"Incredible," he murmured, lying close by her again, his fingers slowly wandering over her as if magnetized to her skin. "I've been waiting so long to see you like this, to be with you." He raised himself up on one elbow, his eyes glowing with desire. "Ever since I saw you I've wanted you," he said, the quiet huskiness of his voice another caress. "I've wanted to love all of you, every inch."

"Drew..." she murmured, a responsive urge of quivering warmth spiraling through her as he touched her.

His eyes gleamed then with raw passion, and he moved his body to meld it with hers. "Say that again," he whispered.

He was above her now, and her body arched to meet his. "Drew," she said again in almost a whimper as his lips bent to claim her body once again. With lips, tongue, hands, he moved over her, always returning to kiss her, drinking deeply of her mouth, then touching and teasing her again, finding the most private places to bring, trembling, to a peak of arousal.

A thousand times, it seemed, she hovered on the brink of ecstasy, thinking she could no longer stand the alternately tender and more forceful caresses and kisses he was slowly devouring her with. She was aware, fleetingly, that he was purposefully holding himself back, that he was leading her, yet seeming to let her lead him, to still another plateau of exquisite rapture.

At last she could stand it no longer. Her hands moved everywhere upon him, pulling him closer, pulling him in as she arched up to him, opening herself to him with a cry of longing. He entered her then, groaning himself, kissing her fiercely, exultantly, as she gave herself over to the mounting, quickening wave of euphoria, wrapping her body around his. She felt him move within her, move with her, and they were moving as one in a slow, suspended eternity of exhilarating rapture. She clung to him, hearing him call her name as if from a distance as their bodies shifted rhythm, synchronizing, rocking faster, faster still, until there was all motion and no motion and the sunlight was brightening, a fiery, spiraling nova within her and without her and she arched one final time beneath him and was launched, flying into that white light of purest ecstasy.

For the longest moment she flew in the white light, then the falling began, a weightless falling through warm darkness. She held on to him as she descended, her body shaking uncontrollably, and then the shivering subsided, and she felt his skin, vibrantly warm against hers, smelled the salty-sweet muskiness of him enveloping her, tasted him on her tongue and felt the achingly lovely roughness of his whiskers against her cheek. Her cheeks were wet. She realized, as her eyes slowly opened, that she had cried.

His eyes, hooded with passion's aftermath, gazed into hers beneath long lashes, a simmering heat in the turquoise depths mirroring her own. "Hi, there," he murmured, and he kissed her once, gently, then studied her face again.

She was so overwhelmed by having experienced the peak of pleasure that she was unable to speak, but gazed back up at him, wondering if he could tell that she had just disintegrated into minute particles and then been miraculousy reformed into the same woman, but somehow very, very different.

"Let me take this opportunity," he said softly, the hint of a roguish grin nudging up the corners of his mouth, "to tell you that you are the most heart-rendingly beautiful woman I've ever seen in my short—and up until now, never this happy—life. Also, I might add, the most difficult."

"Oh?" she whispered dreamily. It was all she could come back with.

"I've enjoyed fighting you, but now that I've made love with you, the fighting has lost its luster. What do you think?"

"I don't. Can't," she said, and took a deep breath, then exhaled slowly. She was coming back to earth, but, surprisingly, the shame, the disappointment, the sense of loss she'd often felt after sex in the past was blissfully absent. Instead, she felt abnormally light-headed, and abnormally heavy with exhaustion at the same time.

"Do you think we might be friends?"

"Huh?" That startled her into movement. She struggled to sit upright, then felt a searing sense of disappointment as he slipped from within her. "Oh—I didn't mean to . . ." Her voice trailed off, and she felt the blood rise in her cheeks as he looked at her, sitting back on his haunches. She wanted to pull the sheets over her nakedness, but there was no sheet. That is, the bed was still made. They hadn't bothered, in the heat of passion, to properly get into it.

"You don't have to be so shy."

She realized she was covering herself with her arms, and her blush deepened. He was right, of course, and she slowly let her arms drop.

"I'm just not used to . . . this," she said. The frank appreciation she felt radiating from his eyes made her feel less naked. No, she corrected herself, truly naked, but in a good way. "I mean . . . I mean that I'm not used to hopping into— onto—beds with men I barely know."

"You know me," he said, and the sensuous undertone in his voice sent a little shiver up her spine.

"I guess I do," she said. She smiled. He smiled. And then she was in his arms again. They rolled together on the bed, touching and caressing each other again, until lying still for a moment, he behind her, his arms wrapped around her, he kissed her ear and neck.

"I'd like to know you some more," he growled.

"Umm," she said, cuddling closer into his warm, amazingly comfortable frame. Then a sudden horrifying thought caused her to bolt from his arms. She scrambled from the bed.

"My God, Sabrina, what's up?"

"Where's your phone?"

Drew stretched out on the quilted comforter, pointing at a bedside night table of black ebony right next to her. Sabrina grabbed the receiver and quickly pushed a series of buttons.

"Carrie? It's me, Sabrina. Ring me through to Lydia, will you?"

Drew nodded, comprehending, and as she waited, he rose. Pulling back the quilt and sheets, he indicated she should sit in comfort. Sabrina sat down on the bed, absently pulling the covers over her legs.

"Well, it's about time," came Lydia's gravelly voice.

"I'm really sorry, Lydia," she began, contrite. "I can't believe I left you with those phones—"

"No, no, no," said Lydia impatiently. "I mean it's about time you let that man carry you off into his bedroom."

"What?" she exclaimed. Drew paused in the act of sliding under the covers next to her.

"Well, I was wondering where you'd run off to, and then I did happen to catch a glimpse of someone who looked a lot like you being carried across a room by someone who looked a lot like Drew—"

"Lydia!" she cried, turning crimson at the thought. "You looked out the— How much did you see?"

"Oh," she said airily, "just that. It's not *all* windows over there, you know. But, of course, you know—don't you?"

"Lydia," she said evenly, struggling to rein in her hysteria. "Just— Well, just . . . wait. I'll be back in the office in a minute."

"Not on your life, young lady," Lydia said sternly. "You show up here and I'll kick your rump on out again. Don't be silly. Live it up once, for goodness' sake!"

Sabrina opened her mouth, then shut it. Drew watched her, leaning back against the pillows, his arms behind his head, a bemused expression on his face.

"Sabrina? Are you there? Are you—is there something . . . going on?"

There was such an unmistakably prurient interest in her senior partner's tone that Sabrina could only look helplessly at Drew, not knowing whether to laugh or to scream. Before she could stop him, he'd grabbed the phone from her.

"Afternoon, Mrs. Evans," he said congenially into the mouthpiece as Sabrina frantically attempted to wrestle the receiver away from him. He listened, nodding, fending Sabrina off with one hand and trying not to laugh. "Fine. I'll do that." He grinned at Sabrina, relinquishing the phone. When she clapped it to her ear, Lydia was already gone.

"Well?" She glared at him.

"Well, your boss says if you don't stay right where you are, she'll dock you a week's salary. I'm supposed to see to it you comply."

"Great," said Sabrina. "That's ah . . . ah . . . aaaah—" She sneezed. Drew produced a tissue from a drawer in the night table.

"Especially with that cold of yours," he said with mock gravity. "You're obviously not over it yet. You really should stay in bed."

"Well, Mr. Dalton, we've just gone national," she said, lying back, the crumpled tissue in hand.

"Meaning?"

"I'm sure that even as we speak, word of this...liaison is speeding westward, as Lydia talks to my mom."

Drew shrugged, slipping an arm around her and moving her closer under the covers. "Romance," he corrected her. "Remember? As I said..."

"Yes, yes," she said irritably. "You've been awfully sure of yourself, you know that?"

"Let's just say I've had the courage of my convictions," he said, kissing her on the tip of her nose and then on each eyelid.

"I still think you're an insufferably arrogant egotist," she grumbled. "And I think—I think..." Thought was beginning to be difficult again. Drew's deft hands were working their magic on her immediately responsive body. A shuddering sigh of pleasure escaped her pursed lips. She gazed at Drew, his face only inches away from her on the fluffy down pillow. "I think you do amazing things to me," she finished, her hands starting to match his caresses with her own.

"And you to me," he breathed.

"Really?"

"Uh-huh," he said in a deep rumble of assent.

"I'm glad," she murmured. "Because..." She paused, and then the truth tumbled out of her as she relaxed, beginning to trust the gentle sureness of his touch. "Because I've never felt quite so...ummmph!" she breathed, as his fingers discovered a hitherto unknown erotic zone of hers beneath the covers. "And I was hoping you felt it was..."

"Special?" he supplied. "Yes, it was extra special."

The earnest conviction in his voice provoked an odd, bittersweet tug of some indefinable emotion in the pit of her stomach, and the loving look in his eyes drew honesty out of her before she could think of censoring herself. "I've never felt like that," she admitted softly.

"Not ever?"

She sensed the question within his question. "Not with Wayne, no...Although after a while sex was about the only good thing we had going, it was never this..." Her words trailed off, her mouth falling slack as his hands raised goose bumps on her thighs. "This... good," she murmured. Her eyes began to close as he kissed her again. The room was already growing darker with the sun's descent, and she realized dimly that if she didn't move now, his heavenly caresses would keep her in the bed indefinitely.

"I should get up," she whispered.

"Try," he whispered back, and his tongue darted out to flick a shiver-provoking circle around her ear.

On second thought, maybe she wasn't in quite such a hurry. "Don't you have something important to do?" she murmured. "Like write another book before the end of the afternoon?"

He bit her earlobe. "Very funny," he muttered. "No, I've already done the most important thing..." His lips traveled down her neck.

"It really did feel fantastic," she whispered.

"You are," he murmured. "Fantastic."

"You don't think..."

"Hmm?"

"You don't think that maybe it was... a fluke, do you?"

He looked at her, the deep blue eyes glowing with a burgeoning warmth of desire. "Not a fluke," he told her, shaking his head.

"You mean, we could..."

"Feel that good again? We could feel even better."

Her eyes widened. "You think so?"

He grinned. "I'm about to convince you," he said.

And even as their lips met before their bodies began to re-entwine and it was just their faces touching on the pillow, she was already convinced.

8

OUTSIDE DREW'S BEDROOM window the sun was just rising across the river, bronzing the brown water tower on the rooftop nearby. In the pale rose morning light Sabrina gazed at the sleeping man beside her. Snoring softly, uncombed hair falling over his eyes, one muscular arm outstretched across the pillow, Drew Dalton was as powerful a presence in repose as he had been...

... last night. Sabrina sat up, still and silent in the bed. Though her skin seemed to tingle with a thousand caresses, and her lips to quiver still from countless kisses, she was cold suddenly in the unfamiliar room. The echoes of their laughter, their whispered endearments, the conversations in the dark, and the little cries of passion retreated now in her memory. In the quiet, alone, the whirrings of her worried mind were all she could hear.

She'd been a fool. She'd revealed too much, thought too little; she'd given so much away and he—well, he had given his all, surely, as a lover. Thoughts of his prowess, his ability to drive her beyond any limits of pleasure she'd ever conceived of and then continue, bringing them both to higher plateaus of passion, brought color to her cheeks even now. In a way, she felt she had never been loved before until last night, never like that. But that wasn't *love*, was it?

Fun. It had been an adventure, a wild interlude, almost a fantasy—but here it was morning, and she had to put it behind her. She had to gather her wits, pull herself out; she had to put her feet back on the ground, she had to—

—feed her cat. This simple, pragmatic thought galvanized her into action. Poor Van Dyke was probably frantic, hungry, and lonely in that little studio across town. Sabrina slowly, and with painstaking stealth, slipped out of the bed. Drew snored on. So far, so good.

Her clothes were still strewn in an abandoned heap by the bed. The night before—well, the afternoon, really, which had blended into night—they'd stayed in, to understate it. Drew had ordered some food from a French restaurant around the corner when sometime toward midnight they'd come to the realization they were ravenously hungry for something other than each other. They had dined by candlelight in his little alcove, an odd combination of paper-plate-and-napkin haste with the beautifully prepared elegance of lamb in wine sauce and a vintage champagne. Then it was back to the bedroom again. Shy with Drew at first, she'd become insatiable for him and the pleasure he gave her. Time, and the rest of the world outside, had disappeared for a magic night.

But with dawn the dream seemed over. She was fleeing, like a criminal from the scene of a crime, their arena of intimacy. It was important, though she didn't know why, that she get out fast, and without Drew waking. But when she was nearly finished dressing, having decided to shower at home and change, before work, his sleepy voice broke the silence of the bedroom.

"Hi, there, you."

She turned, startled, fingers buttoning her blouse, nervously pulling it closed as she saw him, lazily stretching in the tangle of sheets.

"Hi," she said. "I didn't want to wake you."

"Why not?" He glanced at the night table. "Little early for work, isn't it?"

"I have to go back across town and feed Van Dyke. What are you—" He was pulling her back into the bed with amazing agility and speed for a man who still looked more than half asleep. Though she struggled to remain upright, it was no use. Then, as Drew's lips claimed hers, and the musky masculine scent of him enveloped her, and the lines of his body fit themselves to hers so easily, she felt it again, that feeling.

As her lips parted, as her blood pounded in response to the lazy, sensuous caress of his silken tongue, as her skin came to vibrant life beneath his gentle touch, the sensation came back to her—an aching, urgent need, a nearly violent hunger to have his arms around her, a fierce longing that frightened her with its intensity. The hands she'd put out against his chest to push him away settled around his neck, and before she knew it, the blouse she'd buttoned was undone again.

"Drew, I've got a starving cat to take care of," she murmured weakly, coming up for air.

His eyes, hooded with a sexy sleepiness, widened in mock outrage. "But *I'm* starving."

"No time for breakfast," she said, deliberately ignoring his intended meaning, and with a superhuman effort she broke from his embrace and clambered to the edge of the bed.

"Then what are you doing for lunch?" he queried, stifling a yawn.

"Probably spending it on the telephone," she said, her blouse fully buttoned, finally. She stood, straightening her stockings. "Something tells me we're going to have an overload on our hands."

"You will," said Drew. He got out of bed. Sabrina watched him put on his terry-cloth robe. But the sight of his beautiful brawny nakedness was slowing her down again. She turned away, searching for her shoes. They were under the bed.

"What have you done about computerizing?" he asked when she emerged, a shoe in each hand.

"We're still working on it," she admitted. "There's been a slight cash-flow problem."

"You're going to need a good working system now more than ever," he mused. "You should really have it yesterday, if not sooner."

"Can't have everything," she said with forced breeziness. "Well! I don't believe I hung up my coat when I first came in, so it must still be—"

"Living room," he said. She turned, and he followed her out into the already brightening expanse of beige walls and blond wood. "Look," Drew went on. "Seriously, if you don't start computerizing immediately, you're never going to get a jump on things over there. It's a perfect time to reorganize, as your expansion goes into overdrive."

Sabrina had located her coat and was putting it on. "Drew," she said in a mildly testy tone. "Isn't it a bit early in the day to start in on this stuff? I told you, we can't afford any new equipment just yet."

"Well, if you needed a loan..."

Sabrina stared at him, frozen in the act of putting on her scarf. "Maybe I should pretend I didn't hear you say that," she said.

Drew looked back at her, unperturbed. "Why?"

"Because I'd like to think you weren't that...that—"

"What?"

"Stupid!" she fumed. "Crass! Oh, why should I assume you'd know me better than that!" she said crossly, throwing one scarf end over her shoulder. "Just because we . . ."

"What do you mean?" he frowned. "I was only—"

"What is this, the high-tech version of the same old line?—Hey, baby, you were wonderful; here, have a computer—"

"Sabrina." Drew scowled. "That's not at all what I—"

"No? It sounds like a classic routine to me!" she said hotly. "Well, it's all right, Drew, you don't have to buy me. You had me, no strings—and that's the only way I go. I don't want anything from you, and I think it's downright insulting for you to assume that I would even—"

"You're insulting both of us!" he thundered, cutting her off. "You know that's not what I meant, and you know last night meant more to me than the sort of stereotypical cheap cliché you're trying to pin on it!"

"I've got to go," she said grimly, and she started to walk by him. But Drew stopped her in mid-stride. His hands grasping her tightly by the shoulders, he stared into her eyes.

"Why are you trying to make a mockery of this?" he asked more quietly, but the intensity in his gaze undiminished. "You've got no reason to, unless—" Suddenly a strange light came into his eyes, his gaze probing deeply into hers. "Unless it's your last defense," he said softly, wonderingly.

"I don't know what you're talking about," Sabrina cried, trying to shake herself loose. "Let me go."

"That's what you said yesterday," he observed, and an impish gleam lit up his features. "But you know full well . . ."

He had relaxed his grip enough for her to break free. "All I know is you're an insufferable, overbearing, egotistical—"

"Yes, yes, fine," he said absently, a strangely triumphant grin on his face. "What are you doing for dinner?"

"Forget it," she exclaimed, striding past him for the elevator. She jabbed the button, feeling her heart pound in her ears. The truth in what he'd left unsaid was hovering around her like a swarm of phantasmagorical bees. "You know," whispered a buzzing chorus of phantom voices. "You know you know..."

The elevator was there at last. She stepped into it, not looking back, not wanting to see him. She felt as if she were suffocating. But when finally she was in the lobby, then stalking into the crisp cold air, alone, on the empty street, she couldn't ignore the word that plagued her at her heels. It was the word for that strange, unsettling, exquisitely delicious feeling she'd been feeling, and could feel even now.

"All right!" she exclaimed to the sun, to the sidewalk, and to the impassive buildings that surrounded her. "Maybe it's true, heaven help me—maybe I *am* in love!"

Fortunately Lydia didn't have a chance to deluge Sabrina with questions about her night at Drew's; she was dealing with another sort of deluge herself when Sabrina showed up, bright and early, after having quickly fed the indignant Van Dyke, showered, and changed. The first mound of mail in response to the *Personality* article had arrived.

Along with the usual speaker evaluations, correspondence, and incoming checks and bills, there were so many queries—most with résumés and clippings enclosed—from prospective clients, that Lydia and Sabrina had a huge stack apiece to sort through. The phones continued to ring practically nonstop.

For the first time in their few years of business they felt perilously understaffed. A temporary secretary was called in to handle the phone traffic, while Carrie was relegated to typing responses and organizing mailings. Even with all hands on deck—Lucy pitched in, spending some time away from her books to create new files for accounts that were coming in hourly—Sabrina felt swamped. She and Lydia developed a shorthand code for communicating in the midst of phone calls, so that most of their conversation that day consisted of half sentences, like "American Contractors want

Farrington, March," "I sold Vanessa to Merrill Lynch," "Sony and Andy Morrel, Florida, okay?"

Sabrina refused a call from Drew, feeling she had things well in control as it was, and didn't want to swerve from the high-energy all-business track she was on. But at the end of the day she did accept a call from her father. She felt for once he couldn't faze her.

"Well, congratulations," he said. His voice sounded resonantly hearty from across the country.

"Thanks," she said pleasantly. "You've seen the article?"

"Your mother showed it to me last night," he said. "Seems you and Lydia are making a name for yourselves."

"Things are picking up," she admitted.

"You must be getting quite a response. Mother tells me that a plug like that could equal fifty new accounts easily."

"It looks that way." She was beaming, in spite of herself. It was unlike her father to bestow such lavish praise.

"I guess it pays to have a man like that Dalton fellow on your side," he went on.

"Yes," she said, a little more guardedly. How much, she wondered, had he been in communication with her mother?

There was a pregnant pause. "At any rate, I suppose the Evans office is about to expand. You'll probably need to hire an account executive within the year, won't you?"

Sabrina sighed. She'd been hoping he wouldn't start in with one of his "suggestions," but she could hear his ever-persistent voice of authority gearing up. "We might, Father," she said cautiously. "Don't worry, Lydia and I have everything in hand."

"Is that Lucy woman working full-time for you yet?"

"Not yet, but, really, Father, why does it concern—"

"You know, John Cotton works at a New York firm now. If you find you need a little extra help, I'm sure he'd be glad—"

"Father, please!" she interrupted sharply. "Honestly, we don't need any assistance from your old accountant. We do have our own."

"Well, I was only suggesting, Sabrina—"

"Dad?" The rarely used word came out almost as a plea. "Do you think that just this once you could give me credit for having managed pretty well on my own? Without your help?"

The line crackled and was briefly silent. Then her father chuckled. "You're absolutely right, Sabrina," he said with gruff good humor. "You have managed quite well, and I'm... I'm happy to see that you're a success," he concluded.

"Good," she said, genuinely grateful that he'd conceded this all-important point. "I appreciate your calling, but we are awfully busy here, so..."

"I just wanted you to know that I'm here if you need anything."

"I know you are," she said. "Thanks again." She hung up with a sigh, a little black cloud hanging over her for the first time that day. She rubbed her eyes. How like Dad, she mused. He gave a compliment and took it away in the same breath. Sabrina sighed. Well, perhaps his intentions had been good. He probably couldn't help himself. A man like Charles Hamilton was so used to taking over...

She found herself staring at the window blinds, thinking suddenly of *him*. Her last conversation with Drew came back to her. Why did all the men in her life think they knew what was best for her, think they knew better than she did? Well, you know how to pick 'em, she reflected ruefully. Wayne was in the same mold. Why should she think that Drew was any different?

"Cynthia Coleman on oh-two," said the temp when she picked up the blinking intercom.

Her self-analysis would have to wait for a more leisurely moment. Sabrina went back to work.

She stayed at work, hard at work, for the rest of the week. Drew called daily, and she put him off. Speaking to him only briefly, she cited her doubled workload as an excuse for not seeing him, and, in a way, it was a valid excuse.

In a way, it was torture. Even hearing his voice on the telephone made her pulse quicken. Her dreams were suffused with erotic imagery half-fantasized, half-remembered from their night together. At times in the middle of a business call she'd find herself vividly reliving an intimate moment they'd shared across the street, and a part of her would be there, back with him, while her abandoned professional self would be left to struggle to maintain interest in the conversation she was having. She was tempted to fly into his arms, surrender herself to his desires and her own—but she forced herself to resist. He'd made her feel good, feel too much for her own good. Give in now, when she needed every ounce of control to stay on top of things? Not a chance.

"I'm still up to my ears in new accounts," she told him late Friday afternoon when he called again. She mimed a good-bye to Carrie, who was leaving for the day.

"I know when I'm being avoided," he said. "Don't tell me your Dalton allergy is acting up."

Sabrina smiled. "No, I'm just terrifically busy."

"You're terrifically sexy," he said. "And the thought of all your energy being expended on a telephone and a typewriter when I'm just across the street is driving me crazy," he added. "Don't you ever take a break for refreshments?"

"I know what your idea of a meal is," she said dryly. Lydia was standing at the door to her office, waiting expectantly. "Listen, I've got to talk to Lydia. Maybe we can get together next week sometime."

"I don't believe this," he said. "Are you made of steel, or what?"

"Have a nice weekend," she said, and hung up.

"I'm pooped," Lydia said, dropping into the chair by the desk. "What do you say we close up shop? I feel like we've just worked a month in a week."

"I know what you mean," Sabrina said. "I'm just going to get this last batch of mailings together and call it quits."

"Going out?" Lydia nodded a head toward the window.

"Going home," Sabrina said pointedly.

"Dalton out of town?"

"No," Sabrina said, and tried to convey that she was intent on organizing the folder that was open on her desk.

"Then you're out of your mind," Lydia said matter-of-factly.

Sabrina shot her a withering look. "Not at all," she said.

"He scares the hell out of you, doesn't he?" said Lydia.

Sabrina slapped the folder shut. "Lydia, what on earth gives you that idea?"

Lydia blew a smoke ring and gazed levelly at Sabrina, who could feel her cheeks reddening under the older woman's scrutiny. "You're blushing," she noted.

"Go home," Sabrina muttered in mock disgust. Chuckling, Lydia stood up as Sabrina turned her attention to an unsorted pile of mail.

"Don't stay too late, dear," Lydia said, pausing at the door. "And I do sincerely hope that you have more than a *nice* weekend." She ducked as Sabrina threatened to throw a paperweight at her, and, laughing, went into the other office to collect her things.

Lydia was soon gone, and alone Sabrina continued working. Soon she was so absorbed in reorganizing her list of contact follow-ups for the weeks ahead that she didn't take notice of the noise at her window until it became too persistent to ignore.

She'd been vaguely aware of a rustling outside some minutes earlier, but thought it was the strong wind and nothing more. Now she heard that rustling closer, and a gentle, rhythmic tapping against the window behind her closed blinds. Sabrina rose from the pile of papers on her desk and pulled the blinds up.

There was a huge yellowish blur of color filling the windowpane. Startled, she took a step back, and then the outlines of the thing came into focus. It was a kite, some three feet long and two feet wide, bobbing in the wind, apparently lodged in the window frame. The tapping noise was caused by a trail of ribbons tied to its bottom, and a small brown paper bag was attached there as well to act as ballast and keep the bright yellow contraption in place.

Frowning, Sabrina pulled up the window. A gust of cold air blew some papers from her desk and she turned hurriedly, anchoring the rest on the desk. She gathered the pieces from the floor and returned to the window. The kite had risen a foot or so, and now she could see the long white twine snaking out from behind it.

Naturally. There he was, standing outside a glass-paneled door of his penthouse on the roof across the street. From this distance she could see him smiling cheerily at her, a reel of twine in one hand and something indistinguishable in the other.

"Hi, there!" Drew called.

She shook her head in mock annoyance, unable to keep a smile from sneaking onto her face. In the golden rays of the setting sun he cut a rakish figure in his trench coat, totally at ease, as if he always flew kites on days so chilly his breath formed little white clouds as he spoke.

"Open it!" he called, gesturing at the kite.

Sabrina looked at the kite in confusion, then noticed again the little brown bag. Leaning over her windowsill, she grabbed hold of the nearest ribbon and tugged the bag closer, until she could reach it. When she freed the bag of its ties, the kite flew up another foot. Drew tugged the line from his end, keeping it from flying off completely.

Inside the bag, carefully wrapped in newspaper, was a single wineglass, and inside of it, an embossed card. Sabrina removed the card and read the message printed in Drew's neat handwriting:

You are cordially invited to join me in a bottle of excellent white wine. Come to Dalton's—where the elite meet after a hard week's work. RSVP requested.

She looked up from the note to see what Drew was holding up in his other hand—a wine bottle. A glint of glass in the hand that held the kite twine indicated he had a twin to the one she'd just received.

"You're overworked," he called. "Come on over!"

"I'm still busy!" she yelled back, then anxiously scanned the street below. There was nobody in sight.

"It's downright unhealthy!" he yelled. "If you don't come out, I'm coming over there!"

Sabrina glared at him, her hands on her hips, and tried to ignore the soft surge of inappropriate happiness that was welling up inside her at seeing him again. "All right!" she yelled finally. "I'll meet you in the middle," She pointed at the street below.

"Now you're talking!" he called. "I'll be right down!" And as she watched, he tossed the roll of twine. The kite flapped back from above her window and sailed into the blue, a golden diamond flashing in the sun's last rays.

Sabrina had never before sipped wine from a crystal glass while standing at the ramparts of a walkway overlooking the East River. It was an odd, exhilarating sensation, feeling the warmth of the wine within her while the cool wind whipped through her legs and a tingling excitement at the nearness of Drew.

Other than a stout old woman walking a miniature poodle, they were the only people there, watching a barge glide down the river, listening to the rush of water below and the sounds of distant traffic. As Drew rested his wineglass on the stone ledge, refilling it from the bottle and then refreshing her glass, Sabrina watched his profile in the last orange rays of the sun. She noticed a little nick in his chin where he'd cut himself shaving. She took another sip of wine and leaned back against the rampart. The lady with the dog was gone. They had the place to themselves—the walkway, the river, the city. A horn sounded from the bridge some blocks below. A pigeon circled the gnarled limb of a tree nearby, then landed on it, immediately joined by a companion.

She felt as if all her senses were heightened. She was seeing sharper, hearing clearer, smelling fall in the air, as if it had just begun and wasn't nearly over. She took a deep breath, a smile growing from inside her that she couldn't contain. She didn't know why; she couldn't care less.

"What's funny?" Drew was watching her, leaning on the stone ledge, his glass cupped in his hand.

"I don't know. This, I guess. An unexpected place for cocktails."

"You couldn't make up your mind, remember? We're supposed to be debating on restaurant possibilities."

"Oh," she said, and the smile wouldn't go away when she looked at him. "What are you in the mood for?"

He raised an eyebrow. Something moved inside her, and the bubbling feeling deepened into an insinuating, sensuous pulse. The wind rose suddenly. Even as she shivered Drew drew closer to her, his arm sliding around her back. The shiver abated, but her breath quickened. His face was inches from hers. His hand caressed her cheek.

"What I'm in the mood for," he said softly, "is usually frowned on in public places. But I happen to know an establishment, a mere block or two from here, that has a crackling fire going, more wine, and enough delicacies in the cupboard to tide us over for a while..."

"Sounds familiar," she said, her voice a little tremulous as his fingers traced the line of her neck.

"Let's make it more so," he suggested.

They walked. His arm was still around her, and she settled into his body, their strides falling into step. They didn't say much, though his seemingly casual embrace communicated much, and the tingling, trembling response of her body to his spoke volumes. Sabrina felt as if she were gliding, suspended, though every detail of sky and earth glowed with vivid color as she moved with him. Silent, they entered his building, moved past the doorman, who— or did she imagine it?—sensed some of their rapture with each other, their eyes twinkling as he gallantly ushered them inside. In the elevator she couldn't sense the motion from a rushing in her ears as he pulled her even closer to him.

The huge room was darkening, shadows forming columns as the sky turned pinkish-purple outside the many windows. Drew had indeed left a fire crackling. They walked over to it, staring wordlessly into the flames. Then Drew turned to face her.

"I'll take your coat," he said, his voice low and husky.

He slipped it from her, dropped it on the couch nearby, then quickly removed his own and flung it over hers. "And this," he breathed, his eyes intent on hers. His hands went up to untie the black ribbon around her high lace collar.

Silently then, with infinitely tantalizing patience, he unbuttoned the many buttons of her white lace blouse. She in turn slipped his jacket from his shoulders and untied his tie. They undressed each other slowly, savoring each moment of increasing revelation. Her blouse met his shirt on the floor, followed by his belt. When he'd unclasped her bra, a small sigh escaped his lips. His eyes savored the rounded curves rising and falling, the dark tips on the soft globes stiffening to meet his gently grazing fingertips.

A rosy flush spread through her as he removed the rest of her clothing, his lips kissing each new part of her that was revealed, and she couldn't stop the tremors coursing through her body. A sudden almost desperate hunger overwhelmed her. Her hands tugged at his trousers, impatient, till at last he was as naked as she.

His hands savored her slender waist, her rounded hips, her long, slender legs, and the soft tangle of curls between them. Her hands caressed him, eager to feel the strength of his supple torso, the tightening muscles in his thighs and the hardness of him, the skin hot to her touch.

Drew stepped back to savor her nakedness in the glow of the fire, his eyes drinking in each line and curve of her body as she cherished his. Then his hand came up to her hair. Slowly, carefully, he undid the pins that held her tresses tightly in place.

She rubbed her cheek against the softness of his inner wrist, feeling his pulse beat as he unwound her hair. Her body was trembling, shivering with anticipation. Drew withdrew his hand as she shook some stray curls from her face, basking in his cherishing gaze.

A log shifted and crackled in the fireplace. Sparks flew in the air. With a groan of uncontrollable passion he pulled her to him. Bodies and lips melding in the firelight, they embraced with a desire fueled all the more by their long separation. She felt half-crazed with violent, overwhelming surges of need as he touched her everywhere, and she him, lips, tongues, and hands searching in a relentless drive toward fulfillment.

Through a haze of molten desire her mind reeled, wondering at the intensity of these feelings—feelings she'd never experienced before so strongly, so quickly. As Drew moved to cover her body with his, gently rolling her back against the soft rug, and she felt the sureness of his hands' caress, the power of his touch that intimated wild desire only barely held in check, she sensed what it was in his loving that made such a crucial difference, what released her own passion, unbridled and abandoned; Drew was a lover who took pleasure in the giving of it.

Whispering her name in a deep, shuddering breath, he caressed and stroked her until the sensations unleashed within her elicited wild moans from her parted lips. The taut peaks of her breasts ached with the pleasure of his mouth. When he moved from them to her flat abdomen and beyond, she cried aloud, quaking in his eager grasp.

When at last he was poised above her, parting her legs beneath his, her hands pulling him to her, urging him to enter, he paused, gazing at her with a look that melted her soul.

"My love," he whispered.

"Yes," she murmured hoarsely. "Yes . . . love . . ."

With a joyous groan of pleasure he entered her and she arched to receive him, gasping. Now he held nothing back, the driving hardness of him fitting perfectly, exquisitely, to the soft, yielding core of her, and they moved as one in a violent paroxysm of relentless desire that spiraled, higher and higher in the dancing flames. Together they climbed, racing into the soaring exultation of fiery, exquisite ecstasy, spinning beyond earth and sky into a oneness beyond space, beyond time, until sweet joy shattered all sensation and there was only the warmest, deepest bliss she had ever known.

Later, their faces nearly touching on the pillow in his bed, their limbs wrapped around each other in cocoonlike comfort beneath the covers, they laughed as Drew's stomach grumbled suddenly in the silence and Sabrina's gurgled in response.

"Our bodies are trying to tell us something," he said.

"They've told us so much already," she sighed happily, settling her head back into the crook of his arm. "Oh, dear," she muttered.

"What's up?"

"If we're hungry, Van Dyke must be starved," she said. "But I don't think I can move."

"You ought to bring him over here," Drew mused.

"So he can see how the other half lives? What on earth for, Drew?"

"Come to think of it, you ought to bring some of your stuff over."

"Wait a second, what makes you think there's any need—"

"I'm not letting you stay away from me for such long stretches anymore," he said, and there was a seriousness in his tone that touched her even as it filled her with trepidation.

"That's a sweet thought, Drew," she said. "But I don't think—"

"Wouldn't it be convenient?" he persisted. He sat up a

bit, resting his weight on an elbow. "You ought to bring over some clothes..."

"So I can take them off as soon as I'm in the door?" she joked, trying to diffuse his preoccupation with this topic. "Seems silly. Now tell me, what delicacies are there in the cupboard? You mentioned—"

"You ought to be here, period," he said, and then he sat upright, gazing down at her with a peculiar glow in his eyes. "You should be here with me."

The luminous intensity in his eyes was disturbing her. "Let's talk about it after a snack," she suggested. "I'd settle for a can of soup, or cheese and crackers—or some fruit. Got any?"

"What you really ought to do is marry me."

"Apples? Oranges? Wait a second. What did you—"

"Will you?"

"Will I what?"

"Marry me," he said quietly.

Sabrina opened her mouth but could only stare at him, struck dumb. When she found her voice it came out unnaturally high. "Me? Marry you?"

He smiled, gently tracing the curve of her chin with his thumb. "There's no one else here, is there? Yes, you—and me. I think we should get married."

"You're kidding," she said, still disbelieving.

"I'm serious," he said with an injured air.

"You couldn't be," she murmured, dazed. She suddenly felt claustrophobic in the big, comfortable bed, and moved away from him, struggling to sit upright. "Don't you think we should see if we can get through one evening together without fighting first? And talk about this idea of yours in...say, a year or so? That is, if we're still talking?"

"Listen to me," he said earnestly.

"Let's eat," she suggested nervously, and started to get up from the bed. But before she'd done more than throw back the covers, Drew lunged to pin her down in a soft tackle, his weight throwing her back against the pillows.

"Now that I've got your undivided attention," he said pleasantly, his eyes gleaming, "let's take this a little more slowly."

"Let's not," she pleaded. "You're being ridiculous."

"No, I'm being honest. Why can't you take me seriously?"

"Why should I?"

"Because I'm in love with you, dammit," he said impatiently. "I don't throw marriage proposals around to be funny."

"Could've fooled me," she said, and blanched beneath the fierce intensity of his stare. "Well, look, it's an absurd idea, isn't it? I mean, we barely know each other. We barely get along most of the time—"

"Nonsense," he said, still not letting her up as she struggled to be free of his grip. "I know you well enough to know I want you—permanently. I've had a feeling about you since we met."

"Me, too," she said. "A feeling I should stay far, far away."

Drew smiled. "Scared you, did I?"

"No!" she protested.

"Then what are you afraid of now?"

"Nothing," she said defiantly. "Just this sudden streak of insanity you've developed."

"It is a crazy feeling," he admitted. "But I know it's right."

"Drew," she fumed, feeling an irrational panic seeping into her veins. "Just because we've had a good time together doesn't mean—"

"A good time?" He looked faintly outraged. "This is the real thing, sweetheart—you know it is."

"No, I don't!" she cried, wanting desperately to be free of him.

"You know what you feel," he persisted, his eyes boring into hers with discomforting intensity.

"I don't feel anything!" she blurted, knowing it was a lie.

Drew's eyes widened. He shifted his weight, relaxing his hold. "You don't mean that," he said quietly.

Sabrina took advantage of his momentary loosening to scramble from the bed. "Look, just because we've somehow ended up becoming lovers doesn't mean we have to get any more involved than we already are," she said, picking Drew's terry-cloth robe up from the nearby armchair and quickly wriggling into it. "I appreciate your trying to show you care, but really, there's no need—"

"I'm being sincere, Sabrina." She couldn't see his face well in the darkness, but his words sounded indignant as well as heartfelt. "I wish you would be."

"I'm just being reasonable," she exclaimed. "Marriage sounds like sheer lunacy to me, okay? It's an institution I got committed to once, but I was lucky enough to get out. And I'm staying out!"

With that she stalked quickly from the bedroom. In the moonlit kitchen she opened a few white cupboard doors and located some crackers. By the time she'd removed some wine-cheddar cheese from the refrigerator and was preparing a tray for them, Drew had joined her, wearing a Japanese-style short robe.

They ate in silence by the hearth in the living room. The fire had dwindled to a few glowing embers and the moonlight seemed to cast a chilly blue pall over the room. At length Drew rose and paced restlessly by the couch, finally leaning back against a column a few feet from Sabrina, his arms folded.

"I guess I'm going too fast for you," he said quietly.

Sabrina looked up at him. He seemed so sure of himself—but then, he always did, didn't he? Didn't he realize that marriage was a word that meant nothing but disaster to her? "You're not taking my feelings seriously," she told him.

"You can deny it now, but I know you love me. You said so yourself."

"I didn't!" she said. "When did I—"

"Just before the second time"—he raised an eyebrow meaningfully—"*it* happened. Remember?"

"I don't remember," she said, coloring.

"You're a stubborn woman," he said ruefully. "I suppose you don't remember practically carving your initials in my back with those long sexy nails of yours? That was just *after* you said—"

"I was delirious. The point is, no matter what—"

"You were wonderful."

"—I may have said in a moment of passion, that has nothing to do with this!"

"Passion is right! And I'm just as passionately serious about wanting you to marry me!"

Sabrina clapped her hands over her ears. "Stop!" she groaned. "This conversation is giving me a headache!"

"A classic psychosomatic reaction," he said calmly. "Maybe if we used another word to describe the conjugal state—"

"Any word, any language," she railed, getting up. "You're nuts, and I'm leaving."

"You're running scared," he said.

"I'm walking home," she cried. "I need some air, and you should take a cold shower. All this lovemaking has fried your brain cells."

"Lovemaking," he said triumphantly. "You see? Love! Now listen—"

"Enough!" she wailed, and fled the room. Drew followed her into the bedroom and stood by, bemused, as she hurriedly threw on her clothes.

"I really do want you, you know," he said, handing her her skirt. "And I care for you, and I—"

"I don't want to be cared for. I like taking care of myself."

"Well, you don't have to be so cantankerous about it.

Why does my loving you offend you so much?"

"I'm not offended," she said, shaking her head exasperatedly as her blouse refused to button fast enough. "I just don't trust you, I guess."

"Now I'm offended," he said, frowning. "Why not?"

"You're too much like the kind of man I'm attracted to!"

Drew stared at her. "And you think *I'm* nuts?"

"Look, we should call it quits while we can still be on good terms." She was dressed, moving for the bedroom door.

"You call this good terms?"

"Thanks for the wine," she muttered, crossing the living room.

"Slow down!" he cried, catching up with her. "Look, why don't you wait a minute? I'll get dressed and we can talk this out over a leisurely meal."

"There's nothing to talk about," she said grimly. "I've said from the very beginning of this—this relationship— that a relationship is exactly what I don't want. Things have gone too far as it is."

"You mean," he began, his face darkening, "you're sorry that you and I—"

"Yes!" she said hotly, and tore her arm away from his grasp. "Look, I'm flattered by your affection, but you didn't have to up the stakes."

"Flattered?" He glared at her. "I'm talking about making a real commitment."

Sabrina had reached the elevator. "I'm no fool," she said. As she reached to press the elevator call button, Drew blocked her hand. "Look," she said angrily, "you've been trying to run my business and rearrange my life ever since I met you. I can't begin to imagine what kind of—imprisonment being married to you would mean." She pushed his arm aside and jabbed the button.

"Your imagination's in bad shape," he said in a wounded tone. "Don't tell me you're the kind of woman who can't conceive of having a career and a committed relationship at the same time. I've been through that, and I had higher hopes—expected more, of you."

The elevator doors slid open, and Sabrina stepped inside. "Well, if you hoped I'd drop everything, fall into your arms, and sail off into the sunset with you, you can forget it."

"Sabrina—"

"I'd rather say good-bye!" she exclaimed.

As the elevator door closed she saw the look on his face. He had the expression of a man who'd been slapped. Even as the elevator began its descent she began to feel ashamed of herself. She'd been so panicked by his sudden proposal she'd said almost anything to put him off, not bothering to think of his feelings. When she reached the main floor, she paused, her finger hovering over the Up button.

But if she returned, would she be able to leave again? Shouldn't she make a clean break now, before she gave in and lost herself in loving him?

Sabrina stepped from the elevator. He would come to his senses. That's what she was doing now. She walked resolutely down the hall, trying to ignore the reproachful aching in her heart.

9

SHE WOULD HAVE to get the knack of these weekends alone. Her friend Lisa, the journalist, had hooked up with some European and was sequestered downtown in the Village, probably being romantically, chicly bohemian. Robert, the fellow upstairs whom she now and then did laundry with and accompanied to the occasional movie, was visiting his folks in Long Island. Sabrina was too familiar with the leaden fare of Saturday night television—her friend Sarah had a theory that the networks specifically saved their worst shows for weekend nights to drive Americans out of the house and bolster the economy—and she didn't feel like reading, eating, or listening to music. So she went out for a long walk.

Riverside Park was full of dogs bounding over the sloping, frozen grass, and ... couples. Sabrina sighed, pulling her muffler tighter, working her fingers in her gloves against the stinging cold. Walking with Drew just the day before on the other side of the city, it hadn't seemed this cold, but winter had apparently arrived overnight. Even the spindly, leafless trees were shivering.

After a half hour in the park she was ready for the warmth of her apartment, even if she ended up sitting in it watching the paint peel. Maybe she'd make some tea. Maybe play some solitaire. Give Van Dyke a bath? Only if she wanted to be clawed to death. Good Lord! Being single had never seemed this desolate before.

Maybe she should call him.

No. He'd call her.

Would he?

But you don't want him to anyway . . . do you?

Sabrina sighed, walking down Riverside Drive. She was beginning to feel absolutely adolescent. What was an adult way to deal with the situation?

Rumor had it that adults, at least in this sophisticated metropolis, had casual relationships—whatever that meant. Briefly she considered the option of apologizing for having run out on Drew, and then suggesting that the two of them remain . . . friendly . . . lovers? Was such a thing really possible? Rule out marriage, or any commitment—

"Nothing serious," she muttered aloud, trying out the concept. "Just occasional good, clean, healthy sex."

"You tell 'em, baby!"

Sabrina jumped, startled, as a man drinking wine out of a paper bag on a nearby bench saluted her. She hurried across the street.

But when she returned home she avoided the telephone. Stick to your guns, she told herself. You're better off out of this thing. "Besides," she informed Van Dyke, who stopped clawing the bedpost long enough to stare at her balefully, then yawn, "if he's really serious, he won't settle for any in-betweens. And I don't want to lead him on . . ."

Van Dyke pensively licked one of his paws, yowled once, and walked away, his tail up in the air. "All right," she admitted wanly. "I'm confused."

She got up and listlessly hunted through her record collection for something soothing to listen to. She actually had "La Flute Indienne" on the turntable before she realized what she was doing. Bad idea. It was unfortunate, but Peruvian flutes had to be taboo, due to Dalton association. Were Le Carré mysteries going to be off bounds, too? Forlornly she wondered how much of that man had seeped into her life, and she reflected that Lydia was not likely to be interested in moving offices in the near future . . .

Monday morning she returned to work in a state of contrived composure. Drew had not phoned all the long weekend. Sabrina was now determined to view the situation as terminal—over, *finis*. She kept her blinds down and tried to concentrate on business.

But by the end of the day her fragile sense of forced well-being shattered when she caught Lucy surreptitiously returning a copy of *One Minute to Success* to Lydia. "What are you doing with *that?*" she asked the bookkeeper accusingly.

"Oh, a little research," the usually composed woman said guiltily.

"Lucy's been doing some reorganizing," Lydia volunteered.

Sabrina followed them into Lucy's office, where the two large file cabinets that had held all their client information were kept. Lucy had refiled everything according to topics, locations, and types of speakers, with cross-referencing instead of the more arbitrary alphabetized system they'd started out with. Sabrina had to admit it was a more effective method for instant information retrieval.

"You got that out of Dalton's book?" she asked, annoyed. "Lydia and I were talking about doing something like this just a few weeks ago."

"Well, things have been so busy, you know. And when I read his chapter on step-saving shortcuts to better organization, I went ahead—"

"Fine, fine," she said, waving her hand distractedly. She returned to her office, inappropriately nettled. Ironically she had to call Sandy O'Byrne anyway, a task she'd been putting off. The National Council of Social Welfare wanted Drew for a date. Sabrina called the agent now, to get it over with.

"I'll have to get back to you in a few days," Sandy told her. "Drew's in California taping a show for cable TV."

The news made her feel oddly relieved. No wonder he'd been out of touch; that explained it—sort of... Sabrina hung up, and sat, her head in her hands for a moment. What was the matter with her? She winced as that dull ache of longing returned. Being deprived of Drew's company was hitting her unexpectedly hard. She felt she was in a state of constant anxiety—as if she'd misplaced something unbearably important but couldn't for the life of her remember where, or what, it was.

"Well, if he's not available, we can get them Mike Feibush," said Lydia, sitting down in the chair next to her. "You don't have to look so distraught." She gave Sabrina a knowing once-over. "Or are you taking Mr. Dalton's absence more personally?"

"Not at all," she said, avoiding Lydia's eyes. "There's nothing going on—anymore. I'm not... involved with him."

"Funny," Lydia said, lighting up a cigarette. "You look plenty involved to me." She shook the match out, and waited patiently for Sabrina to produce the ashtray she kept in her bottom desk drawer.

"We had some fun," Sabrina said in what she hoped was a devil-may-care tone. "But then he wanted to get serious."

"That happens." Lydia shrugged. "So?"

"He mentioned marriage." She shook her head. "I bolted."

"What have you got to lose, dear?" Lydia asked quietly.

Sabrina looked at her, watching the curl of smoke rise past those sympathetic, too-perceptive eyes. "Everything!"

she admitted. "Don't you see? Just when things here are starting to boom, just when I'm finally free and clear of any attachments, when I'm calling my own shots, the last thing I need is Drew Dalton trying to sweep me off to the altar and out of my independence!"

Lydia exhaled. "Life gets messy," she said with a wry smile. "Usually when you're trying your damnedest to tidy it up. You love him?"

Sabrina looked away. "I miss him," she murmured.

Lydia gave her hand a squeeze and rose. "Let me know if you have a hankering for a home-cooked meal," she said. "This independence stuff is making you look a little on the anorectic side, and your mother would never forgive me . . ."

"Thanks, Lydia." Sabrina smiled. "Maybe on the weekend."

It was true that she was looking thin. She'd lost her appetite. But when Lydia insisted she attend the bimonthly women's networking luncheon they were holding at Dominique's a few days later, Sabrina recovered it rapidly in the presence of such fine food. Evans, and Pershing, Inc., a management consulting firm also run by women, held such luncheons jointly from time to time to pool resources and have women in business meet each other, expanding contacts.

At the end of dessert, having splurged and stuffed herself for the first time in nearly a week, Sabrina was returning from the ladies' room downstairs and paused a moment at the entrance to the main dining room, struck by a sudden memory. This was where she'd first met Drew Dalton, only a few months ago.

Sabrina scanned the room, feeling a bittersweet mixture of fondness and remorse. She'd been rude that day. Perhaps at the first sight of those magnetic eyes she'd sensed she'd need all her defenses to resist him. She sighed, looking at the softly lit pastel-hued room. And where, ultimately, had her defensiveness gotten her?

Alone, regretfully, achingly alone. Drew hadn't called,

and each day without hearing from him she'd missed him, wanting him more. If she were to see him now, all resistance would fail her. She'd rush into his warm strong arms, reveling in the joy of his wanting her, surrendering to whatever outlandish demands he might make. Even . . .

Sabrina stood stock-still, stunned, her eyes riveted on a table directly down the aisle from her against the back wall. He was here! There, sitting at the white-clothed table, his handsome profile unmistakable even from this distance. She gazed with a quickening pulse at that little streak of silver hair curled rakishly over his high forehead, his impeccably groomed appearance in a light tweed, European-cut suit with wide lapels, a blue and white striped shirt, a fashionably wide tie.

Her heart pounding in anticipation, she began to walk down the aisle. He hadn't seen her yet. He was absorbed in conversation with Harry Sprint.

Sabrina halted in mid-stride, not believing her eyes. It wasn't possible. That he was back in New York and hadn't called was one thing; she had, after all, turned down his proposal of marriage—but to be having lunch with the head of a rival speaker's bureau—*the* rival speaker's bureau?

Harry Sprint didn't lunch speakers to be social. He conducted business this way—and he was known to deal only in exclusive contracts. Even as she watched, the silver-haired minimogul was beaming at Drew as he handed him a sheaf of papers. Drew, nodding agreeably, smiling back, glanced at the papers, then put them in a briefcase at his side.

Sabrina stared at him, a surge of anguish and anger rising inside her. How could he? Was he that much of a cold-hearted, opportunistic, mercenary shark that he would sign with Sprint the moment things were bad between her and him? And not even have the decency to tell her?

Hot tears of painful rage stung her eyes. She whirled around, nearly knocking into an approaching waiter. She moved by him. A quick glance backward told her Drew still hadn't seen her.

Sabrina hurried up the aisle, intent only on getting her coat and getting out. Then, her face ashen and tear-streaked, she rushed blindly into the cold.

By the time she walked into the office she was feeling numb both inside and out. When Carrie told her she had a call, Sabrina mechanically hung up her coat and walked into her office. She stared dully at the blinking light of the call on hold for her, then sat, taking out her already damp handkerchief to blow her nose. Listlessly she pressed the button and picked up the receiver.

"Sabrina?"

"Mom!" she said, sniffling. The connection was too clear to be long distance, she realized. "You sound so close—what's up?"

"I'm in New York, dear," her mother said cheerily.

"That's great," Sabrina began.

"With your father," she added.

"What?" Her voice came out in an incredulous squeak.

"We wanted to surprise you..." She paused and took a deep breath. "We've come on a kind of second honeymoon."

"What do you mean?"

"Well, your father and I have decided to get back together. There are some legalities that still have to be straightened out, but essentially—we've remarried."

Sabrina sat speechless for a moment, disbelieving. Then as the words sank in, she sank in her chair. "But... you..."

"I know it may sound shocking, Sabrina, but after all, you know we've spent much more time together over the past year or so..."

"But why didn't you tell me? You could have at least let me know that—that you were coming."

Her mother cleared her throat. "The actual decision came about rather quickly," she said. "And to tell you the truth,

I was afraid your reaction might be... negative," she went on carefully. "So I did avoid confiding in you when I was more uncertain about things."

Sabrina felt her cheeks burning. "You mean, you thought I'd give you a hard time."

"Well, I know you haven't gotten along with your father. And you don't seem especially thrilled now, do you?"

"I—I just wasn't expecting this," she said.

"I suppose I wouldn't have, myself." Her mother sighed. "But things have changed. Your father certainly has."

"Has he?" Sabrina asked, dubious.

"I believe that age brings insight to even the most narrow-minded of us," her mother said dryly, and laughed.

"Well, you do sound happy," Sabrina told her. "And if you are, that's what's important. I'm happy for you."

"Thank you, darling. I know this may take a little getting used to, but it's a good thing," she finished gaily. "You'll see!"

"Is he—there? Now? With you?"

"No, he's out looking up some business acquaintances. The lack of golf courses in Manhattan is upsetting him a good deal, but I believe he's trying to rustle up an indoor tennis match."

"Where are you staying?"

"We're at the Plaza, dear. Suite twelve-oh-five. And I was hoping you could have dinner with us tonight."

"All right," Sabrina said, feeling overwhelmed.

"You don't have plans?"

"No," she said, and added, to cut off any unwanted inquiries, "What time is good for you?"

"Why don't you meet us here at eight? There's a nice restaurant right in the hotel—oh, and do tell Lydia to call me. Perhaps she can join us there for coffee afterward. I'd love to see her."

"Sure thing," Sabrina said.

"Are you all right, dear? You sound a little..."

"No, I'm fine," Sabrina said, mustering up good cheer.

"I'll tell Lydia, and I'll meet you later, and—congratulations!"

"Thank you," her mother said warmly. "So long for now."

"Bye," Sabrina said. She hung up slowly, lost in thought. "Quite a day," she muttered aloud. She felt as though the world were turning upside down around her.

"Call on oh-one," Carrie called. Sabrina picked up.

"Sabrina."

"Drew," she said, too disoriented to react immediately.

"I've been out of town," he was saying. "But now that I'm back, the first thing I want to do is see you."

"The first thing?" She was remembering his smiling at Harry Sprint across the table at Dominique's now, and anger was beginning to seep into her blood. "But you've had lunch."

"Yes," he said, momentarily confused. Then he went on. "You know, since you walked out on me the other night, I've had time to think about us. I was hoping you'd been doing some thinking, too."

I'm thinking about first-degree murder, you snake, she thought. "Really?" she said. "And you've obviously made some decisions."

"In a way, yes. And I think we should get together."

"What for?"

Drew sighed. "Why is it so difficult for you to confront what's going on with us?"

"Nothing's going on with us, the way I see it."

"Can't you stop being so defensive for even a moment?" His voice was rising, the usual suaveness noticeably absent. "You know how I feel about you. There's only so much—"

"I know more than enough about how you feel." She cut him off. "And about what kind of a man you are. So spare me any sweet-talk or hand-holding post mortems on our abortive affair."

"What are you talking about? Sabrina, you're the one

who's trying to destroy what we've had together—"

"You're the one who's already nailed the coffin shut!" she cried. "So don't try to blame it on me after what you've done."

"Good Lord, you make it sound like a criminal act!"

"Betrayal's a crime in my book."

"Betrayal? My asking you to marry me?"

"What do you call signing our contract? A little light amusement?"

"Wait a second. Is that all you see it as? Some kind of business proposition?"

"Well, I can't imagine you're doing it for love," she snorted derisively.

"That's your problem!" he exploded. "You can imagine anything in the world except the plain truth about us! That I love you, and you—"

"You've got a funny way of showing it!"

"What's more serious than a marriage proposal?"

"Business, obviously." Obviously he'd taken her simple no for an answer and wasted no time moving on to professionally greener pastures.

"You really think so, don't you?" he said in an aggrieved tone. "And here I was hoping I could convince you there was room for both of us to do what we do independently, and still be together—"

"What?" she cried, incredulous. "Whatever kind of ridiculous arrangement you had in mind is impossible. I can tell you that!"

"Nothing's impossible," he fumed, exasperated.

"It's impossible for me to be civil with you, let alone be involved, if you've signed on with another agency!"

There was silence on the other end of the line. After a pause, when Drew spoke again, there was a steely edge to his voice she'd never heard before. "This frustrating conversation is suddenly making more sense to me," he said slowly. "But I don't like the sense it's making. I take it you were at Dominique's today, then?"

"As you were," she said. "With Harry Sprint."

"And you're assuming we were transacting business?"

"I saw you taking papers from him! The only thing missing from that little scene was a hearty handshake!"

"Why do you always think the worst of a man first?" His voice was harsh. "No—don't bother to tell me. But I'd have hoped by now you'd know *me* better."

"I suppose you were just chatting about the weather."

"You suppose much more than you should," he growled. "It's the most convenient thing for you to do, I guess."

"What do you mean?"

"I mean that if you stopped supposing I was only out to take advantage of you, use you, and discard you like that wimp of an ex-husband of yours—"

"Wait a second—"

"And if you stopped assuming that I really didn't care about you so deeply and I'd be capable of knifing you in the back like that—"

"Drew—"

"Then you might have to face up to the fact that I love you and that you're not invulnerable to love, yourself!"

"I know only what I saw!" she protested.

"Right," he said tersely. "Shoot first, ask questions later. Well, if you want to assume and suppose your way right out of this relationship, that's your choice. And for once I'm going to make it easier for you. So long, Sabrina."

"But, Drew—"

"Good-bye."

There was a click. Sabrina sat, stunned, listening to the silent phone. There was a tentative knock on the door, and then Lydia opened it, looking in at her apprehensively.

"My mother's married my father and you're invited for coffee," Sabrina told her. "And I thought Drew went with Sprint but now I think..."She looked at her boss in bewilderment. "I don't know what to think."

* * *

The restaurant at the hotel was an odd mixture of refined opulence and ersatz tropical trappings. Sabrina stared up at the carved Polynesian mask that hovered over a giant fern by their table, then returned her gaze to the elegant silver place setting.

"Have you decided, dear?" her mother inquired.

Sabrina picked up the menu again. "Well, I was thinking of fish . . ."

"You should have the striped bass," her father suggested.

"I hate bass," she replied quickly, though, come to think of it, she wasn't sure she'd ever eaten it.

"Have the lobster then."

"Steak au poivre," Sabrina announced, closing the menu with a snap.

"But you were interested in seafood. Why not—" Her father stopped abruptly, and Sabrina, glancing at her mother, had the distinct impression some nonverbal communication had passed between them under the table. "I'm sure the steak is good here," her father allowed congenially, and he signaled their waiter.

As he ordered, Sabrina observed him carefully. He looked very much the same as the last time she'd seen him—still tan, fit, seemingly younger than his years. The only visible sign of mellowing she could ascertain was a slightly more casual mode of dress. He was wearing a tan blazer, the ubiquitous white button-down shirt but no tie, and the more ostentatiously jeweled rings were gone from his fingers, save one—a gold wedding band.

Sabrina glanced at her mother's hand and saw the matching ring. Looking up, she met her mother's eyes. Her mother, also tanned, young-looking for her age, her hair generously streaked with gray but fashionably cut, wrinkles about her eyes and mouth but still the attractive woman she'd always been, smiled encouragingly at Sabrina. Sabrina felt a sudden compassion for her—it was obviously so important to her that Sabrina and her father get along.

She squeezed her mother's hand in a tacit agreement to do her best, and turned to her father. "How are things at the bank?" she asked.

Her father shrugged. "Just fine. I'm much more concerned about the national economy than about the goings-on at our little branch." Her mother had slipped her hand over his on the tabletop, and he gave her an affectionate smile. "But banking talk has always bored you, sweetheart," he said, turning back to Sabrina. "What's happening at Evans Speakers? That's what I'd like to hear about."

Sabrina brought them both up-to-date on the growth of her company. She sensed her father resist the temptation to offer advice a number of times, and in spite of herself began to enjoy this freedom to talk about her work without being constantly on the defensive. She had a sudden image of her father as a former dictator doing his damnedest to be democratic, and she was touched.

The food was good. The wine helped ease the tension. Only later in the meal did a bit of the old antagonism threaten to erupt. "What you ought to do is open a branch in Los Angeles," her father was saying. "You can't possibly maintain this growth rate with just the one office."

"Well, we've been thinking about it," Sabrina said. "But so far the West Coast hasn't been as important to us."

"How could it not be?" said her father, indignant. "New York isn't the end-all of end-alls, you know. What you have to think of is the—"

"Sabrina doesn't *have* to think of anything, dear," her mother interrupted sweetly as Sabrina grasped her knife and fork more tightly, stiffening in her seat.

Her father cleared his throat. "Well, I suppose," he said gruffly. "You and Lydia know what you're doing. Whoever said a woman couldn't handle her own business?" he offered in a jovial tone.

"You did," Sabrina told him, and the air palpably chilled. "I often heard you tell Mother as much," she went on, unable to stop the long-nursed bitterness from finally rising to the surface. "And it was quite an issue when you left her."

There was an uncomfortable silence at the table. Her father and mother exchanged a glance, and then her mother turned to Sabrina. "Well, if you remember, Sabrina, I was the one who left," she said quietly. Sabrina swallowed, her throat tight. She did remember, but it had always seemed to her that her father's stubbornness and violent flights of anger at her mother's independent nature had driven her away.

"And in those days," her mother went on, "it wasn't quite as easy for a woman my age to get the sort of job I wanted. A lot has happened in the past fourteen years, dear, the times have changed—as have we," she added pointedly.

"I guess your mother was a kind of pioneer," her father admitted. "And I was a bit too old-fashioned to make it any easier for her."

"Not that I was easy to be with at the time," her mother said with a chuckle, and she linked her arm in his affectionately.

Looking across the table at the two of them, Sabrina was ashamed of her own lack of forgiveness. Seeing these once-bitter sparring partners now cuddling together in seeming contentment was becoming less bewildering to her and more awe-inspiring by the moment.

"Is Mother going to continue working, now that you're together?" she asked.

"Absolutely," said her father. "If it makes her happy, I won't interfere."

"At least you'll try not to interfere," her mother suggested, giving Sabrina a wink.

Her father chuckled and rubbed his wife's hand. Sabrina saw a poignantly hopeful, trusting look on her mother's face and a radiance on her father's she'd never seen before. They were both so obviously taken with each other in this second beginning together that their infectious happiness dissolved the last of her skepticism. "I never thought I'd see this day," she told them, raising her wineglass in a toast. "But I'm glad it's come."

"I'm glad you're glad," her mother beamed, lifting her glass. "Oh—here's Lydia!" She waved, and Mrs. Hamilton rose as Lydia approached them. The two women embraced, and soon the celebratory spirits at their table rose to an even higher pitch.

As coffee and dessert were served, Lydia and Mrs. Hamilton traded anecdotes, and Sabrina relaxed in the now tension free atmosphere. But as she watched her parents, the little tender gestures between them stirred a strangely sad feeling inside of her. For a brief moment she almost envied them their happiness. She felt left out of it, estranged from the gay little party. When her father signaled for the check, Sabrina excused herself and left the table.

In the lounge downstairs she tried to compose herself. The heavy sadness wouldn't go away. Sabrina touched up her makeup and walked slowly up the stairs. As she emerged in the restaurant's lobby, she heard her father call her name.

He was waiting for her, by an ersatz South Seas waterfall. Lydia and her mother were still lingering at the table. Sabrina walked over to him, surprised to notice he seemed shorter than her. She was in her heels, but that wasn't it entirely. In spite of his youthful vigor, age had subtly diminished him.

"Sabrina," he said softly, and his eyes held hers, "your mother and I have let bygones be bygones. I'm going to try to make her very happy." He paused. She could see how difficult it was for him to be this direct with her. "I know you resent my always trying to interfere, and tell you what to do." He cleared his throat. "But honestly, I really have just wanted to help. I've wanted—to be involved." He took her hand. "The truth is, I'm awfully proud of you, sweetheart."

His voice was gruff, his hand warm on hers. She saw the little wrinkles about his eyes and the genuine love within those eyes, and something inside of her seemed to shift, give way. Sabrina opened her mouth, not even knowing what she wanted to say, and only one word came out.

"Dad . . ."

The next thing she knew his arms were around her and she was hugging her father as he held her, gently, tentatively, as if he were still afraid to use any kind of force with her. For a long moment they embraced in silence. Sabrina screwed her eyes shut as years of holding back, of defensive antagonism and resentment fell away from her. A single tear forced its way from her eye and trickled down her cheek.

And then she pulled away abruptly, embarrassed to let her father see just how much it meant to her that they had shared this moment. He looked at her, fondly questioning, and as she smiled, wiping her cheek with the back of her hand, she saw that he knew somehow, and understood.

"I'm amazed a woman can keep her balance in shoes like that," he said, gesturing at her high heels. "When I first saw you tonight I thought you'd grown another half foot."

"I suppose you're going to make me go to my room and change them?" she joked, her voice still shaky with emotion.

"No, sweetheart," he smiled, his eyes twinkling. "You cut a fine figure in them."

"Well, we know where she gets her looks," Lydia said, materializing with Sabrina's mother. Lydia nodded in the direction of Mrs. Hamilton, and they all laughed.

They walked through the lobby together, mother, daughter, father, with Lydia beside them. Sabrina had a fleeting bittersweet pang of recognition as she caught sight of their reflection in a lobby mirror. A family, she thought. What an odd and wondrous concept, after all these years.

Her parents were staying through the weekend, then traveling upstate to visit some old friends who had a rustic hideaway in Connecticut. Sabrina made arrangements to see them again, and Lydia made a date with her mother. Then good-byes were said, Sabrina once again restrained with her father, but allowing him an affectionate peck on her cheek which her mother noted with a smile.

Lydia accompanied Sabrina down the steps of the hotel. Small white flakes flurried in the darkness beyond the luxurious canopy and uniformed doormen.

"First snow," Lydia pronounced happily. "And Thanksgiving's still a week away." She turned to Sabrina. "Well, partner, want to share a cab?"

Sabrina considered. "No thanks, Lydia. I feel like walking, I guess."

Lydia nodded. "It's a nice night for it." She started to say something else, then checked herself. "Well, it's good to see your folks looking so well—and so happy. Isn't it?"

Sabrina nodded. A doorman was gesturing them toward a waiting taxi. "You go ahead," she said. "I'll see you at the office."

"Have a good weekend!" Lydia called. "If you need anything..."

Sabrina nodded and waved. She turned from the bright lights of the hotel entrance and headed out into the bracing chill. Flurries of light, feathery flakes swirled about her as she walked down the sidewalk opposite Central Park. It wasn't that cold, and she wasn't ready to go home. Somehow the prospect of facing her tiny, dark little apartment alone was singularly uninviting.

Sabrina passed the line of horse-drawn carriages that always gathered at the south end of the park. A couple dressed to the nines climbed into one, laughing drunkenly as she walked by. The horse shook its head and balefully stared at Sabrina. She felt another twinge of remorseful sadness and hurried on.

You should be happy, she told herself, her heels tapping along the cobbled pavement that went along the park's east side. Your mother certainly is. Your father seems to have grown out of his ogre stage and into something relatively human. You've made a success of your business, you're young, and...

In love, she thought, and that swell of sadness rose once more with a bitter, ringing vehemence in her heart. Funny you should acknowledge it so late, after the fact, after you pushed him away and he—What had he done? Sabrina considered as she walked through the white-speckled darkness, through pools of gold-yellow light cast by the wrought iron streetlamps ringing the park's promenade.

She must have misunderstood. She knew it instinctively, knew that she'd jumped to conclusions, that Drew had been right to be angry. Otherwise, he wouldn't have said what he'd said, tacitly denying he was signing with Sprint, becoming so offended at her accusation. Sabrina crossed the street, heading away from the park. The many pairs of headlights blurred in the steadily falling snow. There was little wind, and the light, wet touch of flakes on her cheek was oddly comforting.

She thought suddenly of her parents. Once they'd been her role model for an unhappy marriage—but now they were reconciled, willfully erasing thirteen years of antagonism and separation as if it had hardly mattered. If love was real, if it ran that deep—could two people transcend even a decade's worth of hard feelings?

If Drew really loved her—if she loved him as she only now could admit to herself she did, couldn't they transcend a misunderstanding? Why couldn't she go to him and find out what had really happened—and if she'd misjudged his actions, which it seemed she had, she could apologize.

His voice on the phone came back to her—harsh, cold, bitter as he told her good-bye. Maybe it was too late, and she'd only be making a fool of herself. She was naive to think she could change things so easily. It was silly to torture herself, even thinking about being reconciled with Drew.

Then what was she doing here? Sabrina took in her surroundings with a jolt of recognition. If she wasn't contemplating such impossibilities, why had she walked through the snow to the street where he lived?

10

SABRINA BLINKED SOME snow from her eyelashes. Down at the end of the block was Drew's building. She'd been drawn here, as if magnetically, while all the while her mind prattled on about her rejecting him, his leaving her . . .

It was all nonsense—hadn't she learned anything? It was never too late. Why couldn't she put her good-for-nothing pride aside and tell him she'd been wrong, that she did love him, she'd only been too afraid to admit it?

The longing to see him again surged up in her—a by now familiar ache that was much easier to deal with than the penultimate sadness she felt at the thought of not seeing him at all. Sabrina began to walk faster, her stride more assured. She'd fought him and fought him, but, after all, he'd won. He had her heart, heaven help her; there wasn't any denying it. And now she'd claim him, call his bluff.

I'm yours, she'd tell him. What are you going to do now?

Thoughts of what he could do, what they could do together, provoked a deliciously apprehensive trembling in her knees. Sabrina approached the entrance to Drew's building with a smile fixed immovably on her face. She felt giddy with the anticipation of turning the tables like this and surprising him with her newfound positiveness.

A glance upward gave her momentary pause. At least from this angle the penthouse appeared dark and uninhabited. Damn! Now of all times, when she was ready and willing to let go, to rush into his arms, was Drew gone?

She hurried in the entrance before the doorman could get to the door. "Is Mr. Dalton in?" she asked him.

"Penthouse? he said, giving her the once-over. Then some recognition glinted in his eye. "Oh, no, miss. I'm afraid you've missed him."

Sabrina brushed some strands of wet hair from her face with an aggravated sigh. "How long ago did he leave?"

The doorman wrinkled his brow. "Oh, they went out a few hours ago. Would you like to leave a message?"

Sabrina considered. What could she possibly put in writing that would express what she wanted to say? She stared at the floor, a wave of hopelessness sweeping over her. The moment was passing. Already she felt foolish. Why should she have expected he would be here, waiting for her? After she'd said good-bye so forcefully, after she'd pushed him away from her so many times?

"No," she said. "That's all right." She turned, forlorn, then was struck by something the doorman had said. "They went out a few hours ago? Mr. Dalton and . . . ?"

"A young lady was with him, miss," the doorman said.

"Oh," Sabrina said. "I see."

She turned, a numbness setting in as he held the door open for her. The snow still fell softly about her as she lingered in the street, but the beauty of it was gone. She felt only cold and wet. The falling flakes mingled with the beginnings of tears on her upturned face.

Home? Where else? Sabrina looked down the silent street toward the avenue where cars and cabs whizzed by, but her vision was blurred by the tears that were coming full force now, unstoppable. There was her office building—a momentary sanctuary. She wasn't ready for people, for bright lights, for the city.

Sniffling, she searched her bag for her keys. She was moving quickly all of a sudden as the pain broke inside her and the tears fell in an unending stream. She hurried through the lobby to the elevator. The door opened as soon as she pressed the button. Sobbing uncontrollably, she got inside and pressed the button for her floor. At first the elevator wouldn't move. Then she remembered to unlock the floor key on the panel. The elevator shuddered and rose.

At her floor she lurched out, nearly blinded by her tears and in dire need of a handkerchief, tissues, anything. The Evans office door was just down the hall. She quickly unlocked it, not bothering to secure it behind her. She half-ran, half-stumbled to her office and pulled a pile of tissues from the box in her desk drawer.

Sabrina sat at her desk, crying in the darkness. She'd never felt so utterly alone. The tears came as if bidden to rise from a deep well, tears from tonight and gathered from all those times she'd forced herself to keep control. Now that the floodgates were opened, she wondered if she'd ever stop.

But after a while her breath came more evenly, her breast stopped its heaving, and she wiped her face dry with the wad of tissues. Sabrina got up and flicked on the light. She walked listlessly from her office to the outer office. In a daze of desolation she wandered about the rooms. File cabinets, she noted—typewriters, folders, desks, and more files. This was her domain, this office, and her work within it, her prize, her goal attained, her precious life of independence.

Not enough.

Suddenly it seemed small consolation. Sniffling, Sabrina

returned to her office for another tissue. She stood at her desk, too tired, too devastated from the long day and night to even move. She had no idea where else she could possibly bring herself to go.

Her eyes wandered to the window. The blind was up, and beyond her own reflection, beyond the swirling snow, she could see the outlines of Drew's penthouse. She could picture its warm, airy interior in her mind. She saw the clean blond wood, the gleaming white counters of the kitchen, the cords of wood stacked neatly by the hearth. She pictured the soft pastel rug, the comfortable sofa with its modern lines, the little tables—the masculine environment that lacked only the softening flourishes of a female touch.

Her mind traveled to the bedroom, spartan as well, but the bed so supremely soft and giving, the down comforter, the sleek pillows where their heads had lain, their faces barely touching, whispering secrets to each other in the dark. And the brilliant sunset through the skylight, and the glowing water tower through the window, which now, as she craned her neck to see, was a somber hulking shadow on the cold darkness of the roof.

A soft noise in the outer office startled her from her reverie. Good God, she was alone in here, with no security downstairs, and she'd left the door open! She listened, adrenaline pumping in her veins, to the sound of approaching footsteps. There was someone out there.

Sabrina grabbed the nearest object of any substance, which happened to be Lydia's glass ashtray. Brandishing it above her head, she turned fearfully to the door.

"Don't shoot—I come in peace."

Drew stood in the doorway, his dark hair frosted with a sheen of snowflakes, the shoulders of his trench coat wet, his face glistening in the light.

Sabrina put the ashtray down. His eyes swept over her, taking in at a single glance her still wet cheeks, the tissues on the desk. She stood awkwardly, facing him, speechless, as the wind whistled outside and the overhead lights sputtered quietly. Their eyes locked. He seemed to peer inside her for a suspended moment. She forced herself to look away.

"What are you doing here?" he asked.

"I could ask you the same question," she said, raising her chin defiantly. "Did you ditch your date?"

"Date?" He looked puzzled. "You mean Sandra?"

"I don't need to know her name," she said. "It's none of my business."

"Well, it's all business to me," he said, a faint smile on his face. "Sandra's my secretary. I did take her out for a drink after our afternoon's work, but I dined alone."

Sabrina felt a wave of relief. But Drew's face was stern. She glanced down, inspecting the floor, where a puddle indicated her earlier arrival.

"I looked up," he said after a pause. "On my way in. I saw the lights, and someone more stylishly dressed than a cleaning lady up here, so..."

"If that's a left-handed compliment, I'll take it," she said wryly, aware that she probably looked like a mess. He was silent. She wanted to drop all her pretenses and cross the few feet between them with a leap into his arms, but now he seemed the one removed, distant, and uninvolved.

"I tried to reach you earlier," he said as stiffly as if he'd had the words dragged out of him. When his eyes met hers, their turquoise depths seemed clouded with anger and mistrust. "I'm not even sure why," he said abruptly, and she sensed the anger was directed at himself. "I've begun to wonder why I keep pursuing you like this, when—" He stopped. "When you seem so determined to push me right out of your life."

"I was wrong, wasn't I?" she said softly. "About your meeting with Sprint. I...I was jumping to conclusions."

He gazed at her in silence a moment. "That's right," he said. "But does it really matter? You've been so intent on belittling everything we've been through together that you've finally managed to shake my convictions."

She stared at him, stricken. She was too late after all—he was backing out! Oh, how could she have failed to appreciate this feeling—a feeling just being near him brought? Even standing beside him in the little office was a heightened experience; his nearness made every one of her senses tingle. The resonances of his husky voice, the scent of his musky masculinity, the liquid blue fire of his eyes—she was painfully aware of all of it, and all the yearning it inspired in her. To be losing him now was the direst irony.

"But—if our being together meant so much to you—" She looked up at him and swallowed, her throat tightening. She could feel herself filling up for another flood of tears. "How could you leave now?" she said quickly, before her voice could break.

He looked at her, his eyes narrowing in perplexity. "You were the one who left," he said, exasperated. "You were the one who said she couldn't love—didn't love me."

"I was wrong!" she cried. Her lips quivered uncontrollably. "All right! I do love you, dammit! But a f-fat lot of g-good it's doing—m-me!" she finished angrily as the torrent of tears broke loose. "W-what's the use?" she gasped, sinking into her chair, the sobs racking her chest. She put her head in her hands. "You open yourself up . . . and you let—yourself be—be—v-vulnerable—"

"Sabrina . . ."

"—and—and the next thing you know—"

"Darling—"

"—y-you just—get—ab-ba-bandoned!"

"Sweetheart . . ."

Drew gathered her up into his arms. Bawling, she let herself be held, no longer caring if she was making a fool of herself, but overwhelmed by the hot flood of tears he'd wrenched loose in her again.

"It's n-not—fair—" she choked into his shoulder.

"Sabrina, my love..." He stroked her hair, holding her tightly as she clung to him.

"You—you think people don't love each other, then they turn around and get m-married on you—"

"Honey?" He lifted her head up, peering quizzically at her.

"And you think—y-you don't love someone, and when you figure out th-that you—you do, then it's too late—"

He wiped her tear-stained cheek with his hand, lovingly caressing the pale wet skin. "It's not too late," he murmured.

Sabrina sniffled. "But you've already made up—your—your mind." she said, gratefully accepting his handkerchief to wipe her nose.

"To love you, yes, no matter what," he said.

She looked at him, still disbelieving. "How—how can you?"

"It's easier than you think, sweet Sabrina," he said, smiling, and he kissed a tear from the corner of her eye.

She rested her forehead against his cheek, tasting the salty wetness of her tears on her lips, closing her eyes, reveling in the comforting feel of his arms around her. "I know I've been...difficult," she whispered. "But I've been afraid of being hurt again. And then, when I saw you at the restaurant..."

He lifted her face, cupping her chin in his hand. "I suppose it must have looked suspicious," he admitted.

"Why were you with him?"

Drew sighed. "Harry Sprint has been after me to sign one of his exclusive contracts since the first day I started working with you and Lydia," he said. "I wasn't interested then, and I'm still not interested. He kept pushing though." Drew paused and looked at her. "I'll admit that when you said good-bye that night I felt sore enough to do something crazy," he said, grimacing. "Sprint happened to call the following morning, and I made a date to talk to him, more out of anger than anything else. Then I left for California to do that show, and by the time I got back, I'd come to my senses. Sandy insisted I go through with the meeting anyway, out of courtesy—and it was good business sense, too."

"How's that?"

"There are many people who would be more than interested in having a copy of one of Sprint's famous exclusive contracts to peruse at leisure—you, for example, and Lydia. I've got one—though I called Harry already to say I'd decided against signing it—and I've also got some interesting information about how the man operates that could be useful to you."

"What do you mean?"

"I picked his brain," Drew said with a shrug. "It's always a good idea to know what your competition is doing, and planning to do. There's nothing unscrupulous about it," he said in answer to Sabrina's startled look. "Anything Sprint would tell me can't be considered top secret. But I did get some insights he wouldn't be liable to openly share with a rival agency. I was curious, and I learned a few things, and it's all over now." He looked at Sabrina questioningly. "Can you fault me for that?"

Sabrina gazed at Drew mutely as a sweet surge of relief coursed through her. She shook her head.

"I wouldn't go with any other agency," Drew said quietly. "Because despite the flack I've given you, I think you're doing a fine job. I've always had faith in Evans. And whether you find it hard to believe or not, I'm not the sort of man who would go back on a deal because of"—he paused, his gaze holding hers a moment—"because of personal differences," he finished.

"Drew," she began, unable to bear the look in his eyes. But then they were moving, at the same moment, toward each other. Her lips sought his and reveled in their crushing warmth, and she lost herself in the shelter of his tight embrace. When the long, dizzyingly arousing kiss was ended, she opened her eyes again, resting her head on his shoulder.

"I didn't intend to be mean," she murmured.

"I know," he said.

"I was just so taken aback when you proposed—I couldn't let myself take it seriously."

"I know."

"I was only starting to get used to the idea that you and I could be lovers—and friends. You brought up the word *marriage* and my head went into a spin."

"I know."

Sabrina lifted her head. "If you knew so much, why didn't you tell me?" she said, annoyed.

Drew sighed. "I tried. But you can be a hard woman to tell things to."

Sabrina looked away, her cheeks flushed. "I'm perfectly reasonable," she said.

"Too reasonable at times." Drew smiled.

"Well, honestly, Drew—it has been sudden, hasn't it?"

"I've known you were the one for me for months."

"Months!" She sighed, sinking back into his embrace. "Look, Mr. Smug, I still think this is the craziest, most impractical, half-baked proposal I've ever—"

"I can see this is going to be a lengthy discussion," he said, putting his fingers to her lips. "Don't you think we should get you out of these wet clothes?"

A mere twenty minutes later she was soaking—in Drew's oversize suds-filled tub. The penthouse's bathroom was half the size of her studio apartment. The tub was built into a raised platform above a white-tiled floor, nestled into one corner opposite a separate shower stall, sink, and cupboards.

Drew sat opposite her in the tub, sipping brandy from a large snifter. Little curls of steam rose in the air between them. Sabrina leaned back, luxuriating in the silky hot water and the feel of Drew's legs surrounding hers. His toes flexed at the small of her back and she smiled as he passed the glass to her. The brandy's deliciously soothing warmth filled her from head to foot, and a sigh of pure contentment escaped her lips.

"You were telling me why we couldn't live together," he prompted her.

"I'm finding it hard to remember," she admitted. "If this is a typical winter evening's entertainment, I might reverse my opinion."

"That's the idea," he said.

"This is sinful decadence," she admonished him.

"Wonderful, isn't it?"

"Yes." She sighed. "But as I was saying—" She took another sip of brandy and handed the glass back to Drew. "I'm a woman who's been married—and divorced. The last time I rushed headlong into connubial bliss it was the biggest mistake of my life."

"*He* may have been the biggest mistake," Drew said. "But that doesn't mean marriage was."

"Why are you so dead set on marrying me? We could . . . I don't know, date for a while. Whatever happened to old-fashioned courtship?"

"We've courted," he said, setting the glass aside. Drew sat up in the tub, suds sliding off his glistening chest. "This *is* the old-fashioned way—love at first sight, a few dates, and a proposal. I don't have to live with you first, or go through some trial arrangement. I know how I feel, and I act on it."

"It might have been love at your first sight," she said, "but I'm just catching up. Besides, how do I know you can deal with my—what did you call it?—stubbornly independent nature?"

"Look," he said patiently, "I'm ready to take it all on— you, your job, your cat—the works. I'm not looking for a hausfrau. I want a wife—a partner. That means equality to me. You have your business, and I have mine. So far, working together's been lucrative for us both."

Sabrina frowned. "There has to be a catch. I'm not a good cook, you know," she added, her mind racing to find obstacles.

"As you're fond of pointing out, we can afford to hire one if need be," he said, shaking his head. "Or eat out. Now, don't get that look on your face—"

"I'm just thinking that—"

"If you insist on being free of my support, I'm sure we can arrive at some arrangement," he went on. "If it'll make you feel better, you can eat yogurt out of your own salary instead of steak out of mine. Besides..."

He leaned forward and kissed her softly, parting her lips with his tongue. "Think of the money you'll save on transportation."

Sabrina's body quivered beneath the rippling water. His hand was slowly caressing a path from her thigh up over her hip, from her waist to her breast. "You are...conveniently located..." She sighed. She closed her eyes and drew him closer.

"It's a good deal," he said huskily, pulling her legs over his beneath the suds. He leaned down to kiss her neck, running his tongue over her collarbone as his hands slowly cupped her breasts. The tiny soap bubbles crinkled and evaporated as she arched her back, her nipples tightening into hard little buds.

"Drew," she moaned softly.

"Sabrina," he whispered, then caught his breath as she shifted her hips, pulling herself astride him. "What..." he began weakly, his eyes closing, then slowly opening as she opened herself to him. "What do you think?"

"Think?"

He groaned softly with pleasure as he pulled her to him, and she sank, her breath quivering, against his chest. "Love..." he murmured, "say yes."

"Yes," she answered huskily before she could even concentrate on considering the request.

"I'm going to hold you to this," he said, his eyes half-closed, smiling.

"Please," she whispered.

"You see," he murmured as the water lapped around their melded bodies, beginning to slowly move as one. "One wonderful thing... about our short courtship..."

"Mmmm?" she said dreamily.

"...is all the fantastic things... we have yet to do together..."

"Like this?" she breathed.

"Like this..." he answered, moving very slowly, teasing her exquisitely.

"There's more?" she managed, her flesh shivering against his.

"More," he sighed happily. "And more, my sweet..."

"I'm sold," she gasped as the mounting pleasure rose like a cloud of joy inside of her. "Where—do I sign?"

"Here," he said as his lips came to hers. "Right here."

WONDERFUL ROMANCE NEWS:

Do you know about the exciting SECOND CHANCE AT LOVE/TO HAVE AND TO HOLD newsletter? Are you on our *free* mailing list? If reading all about your favorite authors, getting sneak previews of their latest releases, and being filled in on all the latest happenings and events in the romance world sounds good to you, then you'll love our SECOND CHANCE AT LOVE and TO HAVE AND TO HOLD Romance News.

If you'd like to be added to our mailing list, just fill out the coupon below and send it in…and we'll send you your *free* newsletter every three months — hot off the press.

☐ *Yes, I would like to receive your free SECOND CHANCE AT LOVE/TO HAVE AND TO HOLD newsletter.*

Name _____

Address _____

City _____ **State/Zip** _____

Please return this coupon to:

Berkley Publishing
200 Madison Avenue, New York, New York 10016
Att: Rebecca Kaufman

74

HERE'S WHAT READERS ARE SAYING ABOUT

Second Chance at Love.

"I think your books are great. I love to read them, as does my family."
— P. C., Milford, MA*

"Your books are some of the best romances I've read."
— M. B., Zeeland, MI*

"SECOND CHANCE AT LOVE is my favorite line of romance novels."
— L. B., Springfield, VA*

"I think SECOND CHANCE AT LOVE books are terrific. I married my 'Second Chance' over 15 years ago. I truly believe love is lovelier the second time around!"
— P. P., Houston, TX*

"I enjoy your books tremendously."
— I. S., Bayonne, NJ*

"I love your books and read them all the time. Keep them coming—they're just great."
— G. L., Brookfield, CT*

"SECOND CHANCE AT LOVE books are definitely the best.!"
— D. P., Wabash, IN*

*Name and address available upon request

NEW FROM THE PUBLISHERS OF *SECOND CHANCE AT LOVE!*

To Have and to Hold ™

___ **THE TESTIMONY #1** Robin James	06928-0
___ **A TASTE OF HEAVEN #2** Jennifer Rose	06929-9
___ **TREAD SOFTLY #3** Ann Cristy	06930-2
___ **THEY SAID IT WOULDN'T LAST #4** Elaine Tucker	06931-0
___ **THE FAMILY PLAN #7** Nuria Wood	06934-5
___ **HOLD FAST 'TIL DAWN #8** Mary Haskell	06935-3
___ **HEART FULL OF RAINBOWS #9** Melanie Randolph	06936-1
___ **I KNOW MY LOVE #10** Vivian Connolly	06937-X
___ **KEYS TO THE HEART #11** Jennifer Rose	06938-8
___ **STRANGE BEDFELLOWS #12** Elaine Tucker	06939-6
___ **MOMENTS TO SHARE #13** Katherine Granger	06940-X
___ **SUNBURST #14** Jeanne Grant	06941-8
___ **WHATEVER IT TAKES #15** Cally Hughes	06942-6
___ **LADY LAUGHING EYES #16** Lee Damon	06943-4
___ **ALL THAT GLITTERS #17** Mary Haskell	06944-2
___ **PLAYING FOR KEEPS #18** Elissa Curry	06945-0
___ **PASSION'S GLOW #19** Marilyn Brian	06946-9
___ **BETWEEN THE SHEETS #20** Tricia Adams	06947-7
___ **MOONLIGHT AND MAGNOLIAS #21** Vivian Connolly	06948-5
___ **A DELICATE BALANCE #22** Kate Wellington	06949-3
___ **KISS ME, CAIT #23** Elissa Curry	07825-5
___ **HOMECOMING #24** Ann Cristy	07826-3
___ **TREASURE TO SHARE #25** Cally Hughes	07827-1
___ **THAT CHAMPAGNE FEELING #26** Claudia Bishop	07828-X
___ **KISSES SWEETER THAN WINE #27** Jennifer Rose	07829-8
___ **TROUBLE IN PARADISE #28** Jeanne Grant	07830-1
___ **HONORABLE INTENTIONS #29** Adrienne Edwards	07831-X
___ **PROMISES TO KEEP #30** Vivian Connolly	07832-8
___ **CONFIDENTIALLY YOURS #31** Petra Diamond	07833-6
___ **UNDER COVER OF NIGHT #32** Jasmine Craig	07834-4
___ **NEVER TOO LATE #33** Cally Hughes	07835-2
___ **MY DARLING DETECTIVE #34** Hilary Cole	07836-0
___ **FORTUNE'S SMILE #35** Cassie Miles	07837-9
___ **WHERE THE HEART IS #36** Claudia Bishop	07838-7
___ **ANNIVERSARY WALTZ #37** Mary Haskell	07839-5

All Titles are $1.95
Prices may be slightly higher in Canada.

Available at your local bookstore or return this form to:

SECOND CHANCE AT LOVE
Book Mailing Service
P.O. Box 690, Rockville Centre, NY 11571

Please send me the titles checked above. I enclose _____ Include 75¢ for postage and handling if one book is ordered; 25¢ per book for two or more not to exceed $1.75. California, Illinois, New York and Tennessee residents please add sales tax.

NAME _____

ADDRESS _____

CITY _____ STATE/ZIP _____

(allow six weeks for delivery)   THTH #67

Second Chance at Love®

____ 07803-4 **SURPRISED BY LOVE #187** Jasmine Craig
____ 07804-2 **FLIGHTS OF FANCY #188** Linda Barlow
____ 07805-0 **STARFIRE #189** Lee Williams
____ 07806-9 **MOONLIGHT RHAPSODY #190** Kay Robbins
____ 07807-7 **SPELLBOUND #191** Kate Nevins
____ 07808-5 **LOVE THY NEIGHBOR #192** Frances Davies
____ 07809-3 **LADY WITH A PAST #193** Elissa Curry
____ 07810-7 **TOUCHED BY LIGHTNING #194** Helen Carter
____ 07811-5 **NIGHT FLAME #195** Sarah Crewe
____ 07812-3 **SOMETIMES A LADY #196** Jocelyn Day
____ 07813-1 **COUNTRY PLEASURES #197** Lauren Fox
____ 07814-X **TOO CLOSE FOR COMFORT #198** Liz Grady
____ 07815-8 **KISSES INCOGNITO #199** Christa Merlin
____ 07816-6 **HEAD OVER HEELS #200** Nicola Andrews
____ 07817-4 **BRIEF ENCHANTMENT #201** Susanna Collins
____ 07818-2 **INTO THE WHIRLWIND #202** Laurel Blake
____ 07819-0 **HEAVEN ON EARTH #203** Mary Haskell
____ 07820-4 **BELOVED ADVERSARY #204** Thea Frederick
____ 07821-2 **SEASWEPT #205** Maureen Norris
____ 07822-0 **WANTON WAYS #206** Katherine Granger
____ 07823-9 **A TEMPTING MAGIC #207** Judith Yates
____ 07956-1 **HEART IN HIDING #208** Francine Rivers
____ 07957-X **DREAMS OF GOLD AND AMBER #209** Robin Lynn
____ 07958-8 **TOUCH OF MOONLIGHT #210** Liz Grady
____ 07959-6 **ONE MORE TOMORROW #211** Aimée Duvall
____ 07960-X **SILKEN LONGINGS #212** Sharon Francis
____ 07961-8 **BLACK LACE AND PEARLS #213** Elissa Curry
____ 08070-5 **SWEET SPLENDOR #214** Diana Mars
____ 08071-3 **BREAKFAST WITH TIFFANY #215** Kate Nevins
____ 08072-1 **PILLOW TALK #216** Lee Williams
____ 08073-X **WINNING WAYS #217** Christina Dair
____ 08074-8 **RULES OF THE GAME #218** Nicola Andrews
____ 08075-6 **ENCORE #219** Carole Buck

All of the above titles are $1.95
Prices may be slightly higher in Canada.

Available at your local bookstore or return this form to:

SECOND CHANCE AT LOVE
Book Mailing Service
P.O. Box 690, Rockville Centre, NY 11571

Please send me the titles checked above. I enclose _____ Include 75¢ for postage and handling if one book is ordered; 25¢ per book for two or more not to exceed $1.75. California, Illinois, New York and Tennessee residents please add sales tax.

NAME _____

ADDRESS _____

CITY _____ STATE/ZIP _____

(allow six weeks for delivery)   SK-41b